Edgar Wallace was born illegitimate adopted by George Freeman, a porte eleven, Wallace sold newspapers at Ludgate C school took a job with a printer. He enlisted in the Royal West Regiment, later transferring to the Medical Staff Corps and was sent to South Africa. In 1898 he published a collection of poems called *The Mission that Failed*, left the army and became a correspondent for Reuters.

Wallace became the South African war correspondent for *The Daily Mail*. His articles were later published as *Unofficial Dispatches* and his outspokenness infuriated Kitchener, who banned him as a war correspondent until the First World War. He edited the *Rand Daily Mail*, but gambled disastrously on the South African Stock Market, returning to England to report on crimes and hanging trials. He became editor of *The Evening News*, then in 1905 founded the Tallis Press, publishing *Smith*, a collection of soldier stories, and *Four Just Men*. At various times he worked on *The Standard*, *The Star*, *The Week-End Racing Supplement* and *The Story Journal*.

In 1917 he became a Special Constable at Lincoln's Inn and also a special interrogator for the War Office. His first marriage to Ivy Caldecott, daughter of a missionary, had ended in divorce and he married his much younger secretary, Violet King.

The Daily Mail sent Wallace to investigate atrocities in the Belgian Congo, a trip that provided material for his *Sanders of the River* books. In 1923 he became Chairman of the Press Club and in 1931 stood as a Liberal candidate at Blackpool. On being offered a scriptwriting contract at RKO, Wallace went to Hollywood. He died in 1932, on his way to work on the screenplay for *King Kong*.

A Debt
Discharged

HOUSE OF
STRATUS

This edition published in 2001 by House of Stratus, an imprint of Stratus Holdings plc, 24c Old Burlington Street, London, W1X 1RL, UK.

www.houseofstratus.com

Typeset, printed and bound by House of Stratus.

A catalogue record for this book is available from the British Library.

ISBN 1-84232-675-9

We would like to thank the Edgar Wallace Society for all the support they have given House of Stratus. Enquiries on how to join the Edgar Wallace Society should be addressed to: The Edgar Wallace Society, c/o Penny Wyrd, 84 Ridgefield Road, Oxford, OX4 3DA. Email: info@edgarwallace.org Web: http://www.edgarwallace.org/

Contents

PROLOGUE

On the afternoon of March 4th, 1913, M. Trebolino, the chief of the French Detective Department, was sitting in his office in a thoughtful frame of mind. His big desk chair had been drawn to an open fire which blazed cheerfully in the grate, for the day was piercingly cold and Paris lay under a mantle of snow.

France was passing through a passive period of lawfulness which was particularly complimentary to the genius of the Italian who had adopted the nationality of France with some profit to himself.

Crime ran in normal grooves, the mystery of the Seven Banks had been satisfactorily cleared up, and M. Trebolino was enjoying a rest. It was the bus driver's holiday for him – no other would have pleased him. The smaller incidents, which ordinarily would have engaged the attention of his subordinates, were, in the circumstances, big enough to interest him, and such an incident now occupied the restless brain of the man who, perhaps, more than any other in modern times, fought crime effectively.

He reached forward and pressed a bell-push by the side of the fireplace, and a clerk answered the summons.

"Send M. Lecomte to me," he said, without withdrawing his gaze from the dancing flames.

In a few moments there was a knock on the door and the dapper Lecomte, fated to take the place of his chief, came in.

"M. Lecomte," said the great detective, looking up with a smile of welcome, "seat you, if you please. Have you heard of a certain 'Crime Club' which exists in this Paris of yours?"

M. Lecomte nodded.

"It is amusing, that 'Cercle de Crime', is it not?" Trebolino went on with a smile; "but I am not easy in my mind, and I think you had best break it up – students are the devil."

"Will it not break itself?" asked Lecomte.

The detective pursed his lips as one who had thought both ways and was decided on one.

"What do you know of it?" he asked.

"No more than yourself," said Lecomte, stretching out his fingers to the blaze; a number of students join together, they have solemn rituals, passwords, oaths – the whole paraphernalia of mystic brotherhood, and they meet in divers secret places, all of which are known to the police a week before."

He laughed softly, and Trebolino nodded.

"Each member swears to break some law of France," Lecomte went on; "so far they have confined their illegalities to annoying one poor gendarme."

"They threw one into the Seine," commented the chief.

"And two of the rascals nearly lost their lives getting him out," chuckled Lecomte; "we gave them three days' detention and fined them each a hundred francs for that."

"Nothing more?"

"Nothing more – their 'crimes' have never got beyond *opéra bouffe*."

Still the chief was not satisfied.

"I think we will put a period to their folly," he said. "I understand students, and know something of the emulating spirit of youth. There is a member – Willetts?"

Lecomte nodded.

"This Willetts," said the chief slowly, "is something of an artist; he shares lodgings with another youth, Comstock Bell, an American."

"He shared," corrected the other. "Mr Bell is a rich man, and gratifies his whims; he is also a fastidious man – and Mr Willetts drinks."

"So they have parted?" commented Trebolino, tapping his teeth with his ring. "I did not hear that; all that I heard was that they were conspiring together to give us an unpleasant surprise. You understand, my dear friend? No gendarme baiting, no smashing of municipal clocks, but crime, men's crime."

He rose abruptly.

"It is time we stopped this amusement – *parbleu!* The Quartier must find other diversion. I like my little students, they are *bon garçon*, but they must be naughty without being nasty. See to that, dear friend."

Lecomte left the bureau with an inward smile, for he was a good friend of the students, dined with them at times and was a welcome figure in the ateliers.

That night after he had left the bureau he made his way to the Café of the Savages – a happy piece of prophetic nomenclature, he thought, for here the wilder spirits of the Latin Quarter congregated for dinner.

"Welcome, M. le procureur!" they greeted him.

Somebody made place for him at the big table in the inner salon. A handsome youth with a sweep of his hand cleared a space at the table.

Lecomte looked at the boy with more than usual interest. He was tall, fair, athletic, with big grey eyes that sparkled now with good nature.

"You have come in time, my policeman," he said gravely, "to hear a fascinating discourse on the propriety of anarchism – our friend," he jerked his head to a wild-haired French youth with an untidy beard – "our friend was remarking as you entered that the assassination of a policeman is justified by the divine Aristotle."

"I am of the Stoics," said Lecomte, "what would you?"

"Anarchy," said the bearded youth fiercely, "is the real order, the true law – "

"And you have pink eyes and a green nose," said the young chief of the police inconsequently, as he poured himself a glass of wine.

"I am prepared to debate that," said the other, when the laughter which inconsequence invariably provokes had died down, "my friend Willetts – " he indicated a drowsy youth with a peaked white face, "my friend Willetts" – he proceeded to illustrate his argument on anarchy by drawing upon the experiences of his companion.

"Your friend also, M. Bell?" asked the policeman, lowering his voice.

The tall man raised his eyebrows.

"Why?" he asked coldly.

M. Lecomte shrugged his shoulders.

"We learn things," he said vaguely, "especially concerning your 'Crime Club.' "

A look of anxiety came into Comstock Bell's eyes.

"That was a folly – " he began, then stopped short, and no effort of Lecomte could induce him to reopen the subject.

Only once did the famous "Cercle de Crime" arise in conversation.

A laughing question put by one of the students cut into the conversation and he shook his head reprovingly.

"No – he did not die. It takes worse than a ducking to kill a member of the municipal police – which reminds me, gentlemen, that I want you to put a period – to quote M. Trebolino – to this famous club of yours."

"*Après!*"

It was the shrill voice of the young man addressed as Willetts that spoke. He had seemed to be dozing, taking little or no interest in the proceedings.

Lecomte, watching him, had marked the unhealthy pallor of his face, detected in the slight flush over the cheekbones, evidence of Willetts' failing.

He had suddenly awakened from his somnolent mood. His eyes were wide open and bright.

"*Après, Messieurs!*" he said exultantly, "you shall shut down our little circle, but it shall justify its name, its aspirations, and its worthy members."

Lecomte thought that Comstock Bell looked pale and his face a little drawn as the drunkard went on.

"Here is Mr Bell," Willetts made an extravagant little bow to the other and would have fallen over the table, but the young man with anarchistic tendencies put out his hand and saved him.

"Mr Bell," Willetts went on, "is the great American, a capitalist, and until recently my honoured companion in crime. But we have disagreed. Mr Bell is too nice," there was a sneer in his laugh, "bourgeoise, by Bacchus! Unresponsive to the *joie de vivre*, which is every good student's peculiar heritage. Moreover, a poltroon!"

He spat the word along the table; in his cups Willetts was a vicious brute, as all there knew.

Comstock Bell said nothing, eyeing the other steadily.

"We – " Willetts was going on, when a man came into the café, and searching the faces of the diners discerned Lecomte.

"One moment, gentlemen," said the policeman, and rose to meet the newcomer. They conversed together in low tones. They saw Lecomte frown, heard his startled exclamation and saw him half turn. He continued talking, still in the same low tone, then he came back to the table.

"Gentlemen," he said, and his voice had a hard ring, "this afternoon a fifty-pound English banknote was changed at Cook's in the Place de l'Opéra – that note was a forgery."

There was a dead silence.

"It was cashed by a student and on the back in pencil was written 'C de C' – that is no joke, and I shall ask the gentleman who was responsible to attend the bureau of the Chief of the Police tomorrow morning."

No one attended M. Trebolino's office on the following day. Willetts was called to London that same night; Comstock Bell left by the same train.

M. Lecomte saw them leave, though neither knew this. Three days later he received a £50 Bank of England note, with no name or address attached, but a typewritten note which said, "Make reparation to Messrs Cook."

M. Lecomte reported the matter to his chief and Trebolino nodded.

"It is the best there should be no scandal."

He put the forged note into his private cabinet and eventually forgot all about it.

Many years after the great detective was shot dead whilst attempting to arrest an anarchist; and his successor, searching his cabinet, came upon a £50 note, obviously forged.

"I will send this to the Bank of England," he said, and Lecomte, who could have explained the circumstances under which the note came into Trebolino's possession, was away in Lyons.

HELDER TELLS TALES

It was Ladies' Night at the Terriers, and the street before the big club-house was filled with luxurious motor cars, for the Terriers is a most fashionable club, and Ladies' Night marks the opening of the season, though there are some who vainly imagine that the Duchess of Gurdmore's ball inaugurates that period of strenuous festivity.

The great pillared hall was irrecognizable to the crusty habitués of the club; though they were not there to recognize it, for there was a section of the Terriers who solemnly cursed this Ladies' Night, which meant a week's inconvenience to them, the disturbance of the smooth current of their lives, the turning of the card-rooms into supping places and the introduction of new waiters.

But to most of the Terriers, Ladies' Night was something to look forward to and something to look back upon, for here assembled not only all that was greatest and most beautiful in society, but brilliant men who ordinarily had neither time nor inclination to accept the Terriers' hospitality.

It was a pouring wet night when Wentworth Gold ascended the marble steps of the club, made slow progress through the throng in the hall, and reached the cloakroom to deposit his hat and cloak, and his inevitable goloshes.

Wentworth Gold was a man who had unusual interests. He was an American of middle height, clean shaven, with hair parted in the middle and brushed back in the style of *jeunesse dorée*. He had shaggy eyebrows, a chin blue with shaving, and he wore pince-nez, behind which twinkled a pair of grey eyes.

He was not handsome, but he was immensely wise. Moreover, he was the type, rather ugly than plain, with which women fall easily in love.

He was American, and admitted his sin with a pride which was about three cents short of arrogance.

He lived in England and liked the English. He said this in a tone of good-natured tolerance which suggested he was trying to humour poor creatures whom fortune had denied the privilege of birth in Shusha, Pa. And he was immensely popular, because he was really a patriot and really American. His great-grandfather had heaved a brick at Lord Cornwallis or something of the sort, and in such soil as this is patriotism sown.

He did not wave little flags, he did not wear a pork-pie hat, nor had his tailor, but the aid of cotton-wool and stiffening, given him the athletic shoulders which are the charm of college youth and amuse Paris.

What Gold did for a living besides playing auction bridge at the Terriers' Club few people knew. He called at the Embassy once or twice a week "for letters." Sometimes he would call for those letters at three o'clock in the morning, and the Ambassador would interview him in his ambassadorial pyjamas.

There was such an interview when the President of a small but hilarious South American Republic decided on aggressive action with another small and equally aggressive nation with a contiguous border line.

The chronology of the day in question may be thus tabulated:

5:00 p.m.	Sr Gonso de Silva (private secretary to HE the President of Furiria) arrived at the Carlton.
5:30 "	M. Dubec (agent of the Compagnie d'Artillerie Belgique) also arrived, and was closeted with the secretary.
8:00 "	They dined in a private room.
9:00 "	M. Dubec left for the Continent.

2:00	a.m.	Wentworth S Gold arrived at the Embassy.
5:00	"	Señor de Silva visited by Inspector Grayson (Special Foreign Section of the Criminal Investigation Department).
9:00	"	Señor de Silva left London in a state of great annoyance for Paris.
11:00	"	Inspector Grayson and Wentworth S Gold met by accident on the Thames Embankment and solemnly exchanged winks.

Wentworth Gold was a professional busybody. It was his business to know, and he knew. And much that he knew he kept to himself, for he had no confidant. He had no office, kept no clerks, occupied no official position, though he carried in his waistcoat pocket a little silver star which had a magic effect upon certain individuals; he had the entrée to all the best people, he was sometimes seen in the company of the worst, and he knew things.

He came back to the hall, passed up the great staircase, and leant over the balustrade to enjoy the spectacle afforded below.

He noticed the Spanish Ambassador with his beautiful daughter, and caught the eye of the Chargé d'Affaires of Italy; he saw Mrs Granger Collak sweep into the hall with her attendant train of young men, and wondered in a leisurely way what extraordinary gift women had, which enabled them to come straight from the mire of the Divorce Court to face the scornful glances of other women.

He saw Comstock Bell and kept his eye on him, because Comstock Bell interested him very deeply just then. A tall, young man, with a handsome Grecian face and broad shoulders, he stood out a conspicuous figure among the men. He was clean-shaven save for a slight moustache. There was a touch of grey at his temple which made him interesting: reputedly very rich and unmarried, he was the more interesting still to the women folk.

Gold, with his elbow on the balustrade, his fingers idly clasped, looked at him curiously. There was a strange sternness about this young man, who returned the greetings which were showered on him with little nods. There was a dip at the corner of his mouth and lines about his eyes which should not have been characteristics of one who had hardly seen his thirtieth birthday.

Bell stopped to speak with a group which gave him a smiling greeting, but only for a little while; then he passed into the reception room.

"Very curious," said Mr Gold meditatively.

"What is very curious?" asked a voice.

A man leant over the balustrade at his side.

"Hullo, Helder!" said Gold, "does this sort of thing attract you?"

"I don't know," said the other lazily; "it is interesting in a way, and in a way it bores one. You were saying something was strange; what was it?"

Gold smiled, took his pince-nez from his waistcoat pocket, fixed them and scrutinized the other closely.

"Everything is strange," he said, "life and the incidents of life; pleasure and the search for pleasure; ambition; folly; all these, judged from a normal standpoint, are strange. As a matter of fact I did not say 'strange' but 'curious,' but the word applies."

The other man was also unmistakably American. He was tall, but more heavily built than Comstock Bell. He looked as if he loved good living; he was clean-shaven, and his face was plump; he had that red Cupid-bow mouth which most men detest. His forehead was bald and his hair was short and curly.

Cornelius Helder was a popular figure in London. He was so ready to laugh at people's jokes, had a fund of good stories, and was *au courant* with most gossip which was worth suppressing.

"What is the normal standpoint?" he asked with a smile.

"The standpoint of a man who is not interested," said Gold.

"I guess that is not you," said the other; "you are interested in everything; a man was telling me the other day that you know more about the funny old politics of Europe than the American Ambassador."

Gold was silent, and turned again to survey the crowd.

He did not like Helder, and he was a man who based his dislikes upon solid foundations.

He was silent for three minutes, watching the moving crowd below; a babble of sound, little spiral bursts of light laughter came up to him. Once he heard his name mentioned and smiled somewhat amusedly, because he was a man intensely acute of hearing as people had found to their sorrow.

"Did you see Comstock Bell?" asked Helder suddenly.

"Yes," replied Gold, without taking his eyes from the floor.

"He looks worried doesn't he?"

Gold shot a swift glance at the other.

"Does he?" he said.

"I thought so," said Helder, "It is rather curious how a man with immense wealth such as he possesses, with every advantage a young man can have, should be worried."

"I have heard of such cases," replied God dryly.

"I was talking to Villier Lecomte the other day," said Helder.

Gold was all attention; he knew that this was no idle conversation which the incident of the moment had provoked. Helder had sought him out deliberately and had something to say, and that something was about Comstock Bell.

"You were talking with whom?" he drawled.

"With Villier Lecomte. You know him, I suppose?"

Gold knew Lecomte; he was the chief of the Paris detective force. It was no exaggeration to say that Gold knew him as well as he knew his own brother; but there were many reasons why he should not appear to be acquainted with him.

"No," he said, "I don't think I know the gentleman, though the name seems familiar."

"He is the chief of the Paris police," said Helder; "he was over here the other day, and I met him."

"How interesting," said Gold politely. "Well, and what had he got to say?"

"He was talking about Comstock Bell," said Helder, and watched his hearer closely.

"What has Comstock Bell been doing to invite the attention of the chief of the Sureté – murder?"

Helder was watching him keenly.

"Do you mean to tell me that you have never heard?" he asked.

"I have heard a great many things," said Gold; "but it is interesting to be told things that I have never heard before, and I hope you will instruct me."

"But," said the other, "do you not know that Comstock Bell was a member of the *Cercle de Crime*?"

"*Cercle de Crime*? I don't even know what the Cercle de Crime was," laughed Gold.

Helder hesitated. Other people were on the balcony watching the throng below. A girl who leant over the balustrade next to him could hear every word he said if she chose. There was a constant coming and going of people behind him.

"I will take the risk of your joshing me," he said, " for I guess there isn't much you don't know. Many years ago, when Bell was a young man in Paris, he and a number of other wild youths started the Crime Club. It was one of those mad things of which high-spirited youths are guilty. Each member of the club made a vow to break the law in some way which, if it were discovered, would qualify the offender for along term of imprisonment."

"What an amusing idea," said Gold. "How many of them were hanged?"

"None, so far as I know. There was some sort of little scandal at the time. I rather think that the irate parent of one bright lad unexpectedly turned up from America and disorganized the society. Most of them, fortunately, had taken assumed names which were inscribed in the annals of the club, and the only really bad crime which was committed was laid at the door of a man whose identity has never been discovered."

"But the man need not have been the forger," said Gold unwittingly.

The other smiled.

"I thought you knew," he said.

"That it was forgery," replied Gold. "Yes, I remembered whilst you were telling me. One of those hopeful youths forged a £50 English banknote and changed it in the Rue de la Paix. I recall the fact now. What is all this to do with Comstock Bell?"

"Well," said Helder carelessly, "I happen to know that he was a member of the Cercle de Crime. I happen also to know that the French police have narrowed down the perpetrators of that crime to two men."

Gold turned and looked him straight in the eye.

"You're a most communicative person," he said, and remembering his known generosity, his kindness, and his *savoir faire*, there was a hint of offensiveness in his tone which was remarkable. "Now perhaps you will tell me who are the people who are suspected by the French police?"

The other went a little red.

"I thought you would be interested," he said.

"I am interested," said Gold, "most damnably; who was the criminal?"

Again the other detected a scarcely veiled hostility in his tone.

"Comstock Bell was one," he said defiantly.

"And the other?"

"I don't know the other," said Helder; "it is a man in the city — a broker or something."

"You are an amazing person," said Gold, and went down the staircase with a smile on his lips to greet an unobtrusive, middle-aged gentleman, who wore no decorations at his collar, but represented ninety million people at the Court of St James.

Comstock Bell had gone into the reception room; a little bored if the truth be told. He would not have come that night, but his absence would have been remarked upon. There was in his heart a fear amounting to panic; life had suddenly lost all its joy and sweetness, and a black cloud had settled on his soul.

He paid his respects to the club president's wife, who was receiving guests in the reception room. A concert was in progress in what had been the billiard-room. He half turned in that direction;

somebody called him; he looked over his shoulder and saw Lord Hallingdale.

"Bell, you're the man I wanted to see," said his lordship, detaching himself from his party with an excuse. "I am going down the Mediterranean next month; will you come with me?"

Comstock Bell smiled. "I am so sorry, I have made other plans," he said.

"Going out of town?"

"Yes, I thought of running across to the States. My mother isn't enjoying the best of health just now, and I think she would like to see me."

He passed on. The excuse had been invented on the spur of the moment, for though his mother was an invalid, he had no intention of quitting England till a certain matter was settled once and for all.

He progressed leisurely towards the dining-room, where Tetrazzini was holding an audience spellbound. The room was packed and there was a crowd about the door.

He stood in the rear rank, and had no difficulty, but reason of his inches, in seeing over the heads of the throng.

"Fortunate man," whispered somebody.

He looked round.

Mrs Granger Collak's beautiful eyes were smiling her bold admiration. Radiantly lovely was this woman of the world, as men had found to their cost.

"Shall I lift you up?" he asked in the same tone.

He was one of the few people who dared be natural with her in public, and she was genuinely fond of this young giant who knew her for what she was, yet never condemned her, and never sought a closer friendship.

"You can find me a nice quiet corner," she said, "for I am bored to an incalculable extent."

He detached himself from the throng and led her to a corner of the almost deserted outer lobby. Here, in a recess under the stairway, he found a quiet spot, and she seated herself with a sigh of relief.

"Comstock," she said, "I want you to help me."

"I could help you best," he said with a reproving smile, "by presenting you with a framed copy of the Ten Commandments."

"Do not be banal, I beg," she implored. "I am superior to Commandments; the fact that they are Commandments, and not requests, makes me long to break them all. No, I want something more substantial."

Her eyes met his, and she read something of the pity that filled him, pity that overwhelmed the sorrow which his own troubles brought.

"Don't look at me like that," she said roughly, "I do not want your sympathy. Have no stupid ideas about me, Comstock; I'm bad through and through, and I'm desperate. I want money to go abroad; to travel for a few years. People think I'm brazen because I turn up here after – after you know. But I can't get away; I'm at the end of my tether. I want to go!" She clenched her hands, and he saw a tense, hunted look in her eyes. "I want to vanish for a few years – to go alone, Comstock – and I'm bound hand and foot."

Somebody was approaching. Looking up Bell saw Helder with a little smile on his lips, ostentatiously looking the other way.

"Come to Cadogan Square tomorrow," he said, rising; "I will let you have anything you want."

Her hand was trembling when she laid it on his arm.

"You – you are good to me," she said, and her voice faltered. "I can't – I can't repay you in any way – can I?"

He shook his head.

He left her with one of her youthful cavaliers and made his way to the cloakroom to get his hat and coat.

He found Gold similarly employed.

"Are you going so soon, my young friend?" he asked.

Bell laughed.

"Yes, I find these functions depress me somewhat; I must be getting old. You appear to have similar designs," he said.

The attendant was helping the other into his coat.

"Business – inexorable business," smiled Gold. "Which way do you go?"

"Oh, I don't know!" said Bell vaguely.

"When young men don't know which way they are going," said Gold "they are usually going to the devil. Come along with me."

They both laughed, and, laughing, passed through the hall down the steps into the street; and there was at least one pair of eyes that watched the tall figure of the young man disappear.

"We'll walk, if you don't mind," said Gold; "the rain is not very heavy, and I like walking in the rain."

"I prefer it too," said the other.

They walked along Pall Mall in silence till they came to the corner of the Haymarket. The rain had increased and was now falling heavily.

Gold hailed a taxi-cab. "Fleet Street," he said loudly.

They had not gone far before he put his head out of the window and changed his instructions.

"Take me to Victoria," he said; "go through the park."

"Changed your mind?" asked Bell.

"No," said the other calmly; "only I am such an important person that quite a number of people spend lives which might otherwise be usefully employed in following me. Did you notice we were followed?"

"No," said the young man after a pause, and his voice was husky.

"I am going to ask you something, Bell," said the older man as the cab turned into the park. "Do you know a man named Willetts?"

"Willetts!" The young man's voice was even and non-committal.

"Yes; he has an office near Moorgate Street. He is a broker, though I have never heard that he bought or sold stock."

"I don't know him," said Bell shortly.

There was another long pause. Gold was leaning forward, looking out of the window and nodding his head at irregular intervals as though he were counting something.

"I think I will get out here," he said suddenly, and tapped on the window. They were in the Mall and it was deserted save for the cars which, obedient to the regulations which govern royal parks, were slowly coming and going along the broad road.

He tapped the front window, and the driver pulled up.

"You had better take the car on to where you want to go," he said.

Bell nodded in the darkness.

"Tell him to drive to Cadogan Square," he replied; "I will go home."

He heard Gold give the instructions, then, before the car could move on a man stepped out of the darkness of the sidewalk.

"Is that Gold," he said in a muffled voice.

"That is me," was the response.

"You were expecting to meet somebody, weren't you?" said the stranger.

The engine had stopped, and the driver was descending to start it again. Bell made no effort to listen to the conversation, but could not help overhearing it.

"Was I?" he heard Gold drawl.

"You know you were, damn you!" snarled the voice of the stranger. "That's for you!"

A quick shot broke the silence of the night.

Bell leapt from the car. Gold was standing on the edge of the sidewalk, unharmed. His assailant was a blurred figure vanishing into the darkness as fast as his feet could carry him.

"A friend of mine," said Gold pleasantly, and picked up a revolver the man had dropped.

INTRODUCES VERITY MAPLE

At eleven o'clock that night Wentworth Gold walked into Victoria Station and took a first-class return ticket to Peckham Rye. He was smoking a cigar, and might have been a middle-aged doctor returning from an evening's jaunt in town.

He walked slowly along the platform to where the electric train was waiting, opened a first-class carriage door, and got in. After he had closed the door he leant out of the open window, watching the passengers as they came along. He did not expect any further trouble that night, but he took no chances.

The train moved out of the station, whining and purring; and the lights of the carriage dimmed and brightened as the connecting rods lost or found the trolley wires above.

The carriage was empty, for it was a little before the hour that the suburbanite returns from the theatre; and he had time to read again a letter which had come to him before he left his flat that evening. He read it carefully twice; by that time he knew its contents by heart, and he tore the letter into a hundred little pieces, dropping them a few at a time from the open window.

The attack on him did not disturb him greatly, though he had been worried as to why the man who had promised to meet him in the park had not kept his appointment.

He reached his destination, descended the long gloomy flight of stairs which led to the busy street, turned sharply, crossed to the right, and skirting the open expanse of Peckham Rye came to Crystal Palace Road. A few doors along he stopped before a respectable villa residence. The house was in darkness, but he knew he was expected. He went to the door and knocked softly, and in less than a minute it was opened to him by a girl.

"Is that Mr Gold?" asked a low sweet voice.

"That is the second time I have been asked that question tonight," said Gold, with a little chuckle. "I trust that my confession that it is indeed me will not provoke you to give me a similar response to that I have already received."

The girl closed the door behind him and helped him off with his coat.

"What is the matter?" she asked, and there was a hint of anxiety in her voice.

"Oh, nothing!" said Gold. "At least nothing more than I deserved. How is your uncle?"

She made no reply. In the darkness he heard a little sigh of weariness, and shook his head. Maple was a genius, he thought, and realized that genius is a half-way house to madness.

She led the way along a dark passage to a little back kitchen. A man sat at the table – a tall man, loosely formed, unshaven, and with a face of unhealthy whiteness. He sprawled limply on the chair by the table, his hands in his pockets, gazing vacantly before him. The table was littered with test tubes, microscopes, and scientific apparatus, with the uses of which Wentworth Gold was not acquainted.

At the sound of the door clicking he looked up with a startled frown. He shivered, as though the noise, slight as it was, distressed him, and raised a trembling hand, not over clean, to his mouth.

"Come in," he said, and rose unsteadily to his feet.

Gold looked at him reproachfully.

"Maple," he said. "I thought you promised me –" Then he remembered the girl was present.

"Get a chair, my dear," said Maple, not unkindly.

The girl obeyed. She was wonderfully pretty. Gold had never seen her before, though he had heard a great deal of Thomas Maple's niece. She was gracefully moulded and dressed in a quiet, well-fitting tailor-made. Her face had that curious pallor which is possessed by some fair

13

women; though her hair was burnished gold, the thin line of eyebrow was so black that carelessly seeing her you would have thought it had been painted.

The shape of her face fascinated Gold. He was a connoisseur in some things. He had read about girls with perfect oval faces; he had met some of the acknowledged beauties of London; but there was in this girl's face something ethereal, something spiritual, which he had never seen before. The big grey-blue eyes gave her the appearance of sadness; the lines of her generous mouth were firm; her chin was delicately fashioned. She flushed a little under his scrutiny.

"I am sorry," he said, as if in answer to her unspoken thought, "but I have heard so much of you from your uncle."

"I am afraid my uncle talks a great deal more about me than people care to hear," she said with a little smile. "He does not know how easily one can be bored with other people's ecstasies."

Her voice was soft and perfectly attuned.

"This girl has had an education," Gold said to himself.

He turned to meet the vague smile of the man. There was a challenge and a question in the haggard face, worn and scarred by self-indulgence. This girl who had recently come into his life, the daughter of an elder brother, and his only relative in the world, was the brightest and best influence he had ever known, and it was almost pathetic to see the entreaty in his dull eyes. Gold nodded reassuringly.

"Now, Maple," he said, drawing his chair to the table, "I suppose your niece is in your confidence in this matter of ours?"

"Yes, I tell her all the things that nearly concern me," said the other, "and you can trust her, Mr Gold." His voice had the quality which distinguishes a man who has known a public school.

There was a little wallet on the table. This he opened with his shaking hand and from it extracted a bundle of oblong notes. They were five-dollar currency bills, issued by the United States of America, and distinguished only from those familiar objects by the fact that each note was mottled green, purple, and yellow, as though somebody

14

had been light-heartedly experimenting upon them. He spread them out on the table; there were twenty in all.

Gold looked at them resentfully.

"And you say they are all forgeries?" he asked.

The other nodded.

"Every one of them. You know the Treasury sign – the only sign that the camera cannot photograph – that is not there."

He was on a favourite topic now; he was interested, and the weariness and the languor of his manner dropped from him as a cloak. He spoke without the slurred speech which had marked the earlier stage of the conversation.

"That I know," said Gold. "What of the inks?"

"Perfect," said Maple, in a tone of admiration, "absolutely perfect. I have applied every test known to your people, and they might have been printed with ink supplied by your Government."

"The water-mark?" asked Gold.

"That, too, is beyond criticism. I have here an instrument that can measure the depth of the printing and I can assure you that they are exactly printed. Moreover, I will tell you this; it will probably astonish you."

He tapped the note which was before him.

"The man who forged this did not have resource to photography.

Every one of these notes is engraven. I know because – well, never mind – I know. They have been printed on a press which has been specially made for the purpose, and the paper is identical with that which is supplied by the Government printers in Washington."

He looked at the notes one by one, shook them into a little bundle, and replaced them in the wallet.

"All my life," he said, "banknote forgeries and banknote engraving has been a favourite study of mine."

He stopped, and his mouth twitched pathetically. Then with an effort he pulled himself together.

"I worked in the French and in the German mints – I should be working in France still," he said with a grimace, "but for – " Again he stopped. "I tell you, Mr Gold," he went on, "that a man can pass this note with impunity and not only this bill, but the hundred-dollar notes I have examined."

"And there is no way of detecting them?" asked Gold.

Maple shook his head. "None whatever. Until these return to the Treasury, where they would be immediately detected, there is no possibility of their being stopped."

Gold pushed his chair back from the table, his hands thrust deep into his pockets, his head sunk on his breast. He was thinking deeply, and the girl from her seat by the fireside glanced from him to her uncle.

Presently Gold looked up.

"Happily the forgers are not so confident as you," he said. "I had arranged to meet one of my men tonight in the Green Park, and in some way they got to know. They enticed him away on some pretext or other, and – "

"And?" asked Maple after a little while.

"And I have not seen him since," said Gold diplomatically.

He was worried. He had hoped that this man, acknowledged by the underworld to be the best exponent of this peculiar science, would have discovered some simple test by which the flood of forged bills might be averted; some simple means by which the forgeries might be detected. He realized now in his growing sense of disappointment how much he had depended on Maple.

There were thousands of these bills in circulation, hundreds of thousands possibly, all for small amounts, all so insignificant that the average man handling them would not trouble to question their genuineness.

"It can't be helped," he said, and rose.

He shook hands with Maple, and took a smiling farewell of the girl.

His foot was in the passage when Maple suddenly said:

"Oh, I had forgotten something I wanted to say to you, Mr. Gold. Do you know a Mr Cornelius Helder?"

"Yes," said Gold, considerably interested.

"I thought you would, he's a compatriot of yours," said Maple, and then half to himself, "I must have met him somewhere."

"He's a very well-known man," said Gold.

"My niece has had an offer from him," Maple went on.

"An offer? Indeed, what kind of an offer?"

"A secretaryship," said Maple

Gold frowned. It was an involuntary frown, but both the girl and her uncle detected it. Maple's hand went to his mouth with the nervous gesture with is the unlovely characteristic of the drunkard.

"Isn't he all right?" asked Maple anxiously: "he has offered her a very good salary."

"How did he come to know that she wanted that position?" asked Gold.

Maple pulled up the chair. The old weariness was asserting itself again. Every word was an effort.

"Sit down for a moment, won't you, and I'll tell you. It's rather a curious string of coincidences. My niece was secretary to old Lord Dellborough, who, you know, died the other day, and she did not intend taking another post because I earn quite enough to render any effort on her part unnecessary. But last week she had a letter from an agency, although Verity has never put her name on their books, saying that the post was going."

"I fail to see the coincidence," said Gold dryly.

"Well, was it not rather a coincidence that at the moment she dropped out of a billet she should have one offered her from an agency she had never heard of, to act as secretary to a man who is, I believe I may say, a friend of yours?"

Now Mr Wentworth Gold had no faith whatever in that eccentric individual, the Angel of the Odd. He made no allowance for coincidence, especially when he could discern without any great mental effort the manner in which such a coincidence could be made possible.

He looked at the girl; perhaps it would be known in certain circles who Lord Dellborough's secretary had been. There would be no difficulty in giving a commission to an agency to approach her. She was beautiful, he thought. Helder had a reputation in London amongst the people who spoke of such things behind their hands in the smoking-rooms. That was one explanation.

He thought of another almost immediately; and it struck him as being the more likely of the two.

He studied her keenly; for a moment noted the clear depths of her eyes and the firm line of her beautifully moulded chin.

"She has character," he thought; "Helder's secretary – who knew?"

"I should advise you to take the post," he said. He took a note-book from his pocket and scribbled something on a card.

"That's my telephone number. There is always somebody to answer it, day and night," he said to the girl as he handed her the little pasteboard. "You had better not tell Helder that you know me – and you had better tell me when you know Helder."

With which cryptic utterance he left them.

MAPLE HAS A VISITOR

There was an infinite dreariness about the Crystal Palace Road which its blatant respectability did not redeem. It was, in fact, the dreariness of its very respectability, of houses alike in architecture and in their very furnishing. White half-blinds covered sedate bedroom windows; drawing-rooms had lace curtains elegantly draped, supported by gloomier tapestry; there was just sufficient space left in every window to afford the passers-by a tantalizing glimpse of something with a mirror in it, and even here the view was usually spoilt by a genteel palm potted in a glaze production of Messrs Doulton.

To Verity Maple the Crystal Palace Road represented a sad awakening from a beautiful dream. She had expected she knew not what, and whether her expectations would have been justified had her father lived it is difficult to say. George Maple, a happy-go-lucky tilter with fate had earned twelve hundred a year and for many years had industriously spent fifteen hundred. There had come a moment when his position was so hopeless that he knew not which way to turn; and he was contemplating the alternative of bankruptcy and suicide, when an obliging motor-bus, before which he stepped in a fit of abstraction, settled the problem for him.

The girl had been brought home from the Belgium convent to find her father's home in the possession of his many creditors. They had the grace to obliterate themselves until the funeral ceremonies were complete, then they returned to save what they could from the wreck. George Maple had been insured, though even in this manner he had been slack enough, for his insurance was only worth its surrender value.

It was whilst Verity Maple had been considering the overwhelming problem of her future that Tom Maple appeared upon the scene. She had heard of Uncle Tom, had received letters from him from various parts of the continent. He had a disconcerting habit of changing his name with his residence; she had regarded this as an amiable eccentricity into the causes of which there was no especial need to inquire. And her father had not enlightened her, save to remark vaguely that Tom was a "queer chap."

He was queer, but he was kind, as Verity learnt gratefully.

Together they took the little house in the Crystal Palace Road and furnished it. His weakness she was soon to discover, but with all its pitiable features it lacked offensiveness, and she found herself living much more happily than she could have imagined under the circumstances, and, moreover, possessed of a new sense of protection, comforting enough, though that protector had the drink habit very strongly developed.

Tom Maple was kind, he was generous, he gave her what she had never had before, an ample supply of pocket-money. There was no necessity for her to work; it was independence rather than necessity which urged her to make an effort on her own behalf, a desire to fill her life with other thoughts and interests, to drive away the wistful discontent that the dullness of the Crystal Palace Road aroused in her.

She had soon learnt to take an interest in the work of this eccentric uncle of hers; she would sit for hours watching his sure hands tracing lines of extraordinary delicacy over the steel plates which lay clamped to the kitchen table in front of him. For Tom Maple earned good money from a firm of banknote engravers, who knew him well enough to appreciate his work sufficiently highly to condone the habit of a lifetime.

She sometimes spent an idle half-hour in the little parlour, wondering what life would have been like had it run its normal course, had her father, whose improvidence she was only now beginning to realize and admit even to herself, earmarked some portion of his income for her future. Especially gloomy was the outlook of those wintry days when great billows of fog came rolling up from Peckham Rye, shutting out the sad sameness of the road, lending to the wisps of trees, striplings that grew gauntly in the small patch of ground before the house, a mysticism and a ghostly importance, which no suburban tree ordinarily possesses.

She was sitting in the parlour on the evening following Gold's visit; it had been a bright, sunny day, and the evening brought hues of orange and saffron to beautify the outlook. Sitting with a book on her knees before the open window, she heard her uncle's light step in the passage without. It passed, stopped as if in hesitation, then came back. The handle turned, the door opened and her uncle came in. She looked up at him.

"Do you want me, uncle?"

His face was paler than usual; the dark rim about his eyes, which was habitual, seemed a shade blacker. He looked at her without speaking for a time, then he came farther into the room and closed the door. He sat down in a chair opposite the girl.

"Do you want anything, uncle?" she asked again.

He shook his head

"Verity," he said seriously. "I have been thinking about you, and I have been wondering whether I ought not to tell you something about myself.

She waited. He looked past her into the road and heaved a little sigh. Then he brought his eye back to her face.

"I have had rather a curious life," he said.

There was no trace of the slithering accent which was peculiar to his voice after one of his bouts. His lips trembled a little, and the hand that he raised to his mouth mechanically from time to time shook ever so slightly.

"You don't know anything about me, do you?" and she shook her head smilingly.

"I know you are my uncle," she said, "and the dearest and kindest uncle that any girl ever had."

He dissented vaguely.

21

"You must not think too well of me," he said. "I am not – perhaps – what you think I am. One never knows," he muttered.

"Never knows what, uncle" asked the girl.

He looked at her a little sadly.

"If anything should happen to me," he said, "there is a man in London I want you to see." He put his hand in his inside pocket and took out a stiff brown notebook, removing the elastic band which bound it together.

"And here is something else," he said. "The other day I asked you for a specimen of your handwriting and got you to sign your name for me. I have opened an account for you in the London and North Western Bank. It isn't huge," he said hastily, as he saw the look of surprise and pleasure on the girl's face, "but it will be enough to carry you on if anything should happen to me."

A hint of alarm was in the girl's eyes as she asked: "You have said that twice, uncle; what can happen to you?"

He shook his shoulders weakly.

"You never know," he said again.

He had taken from his pocket book a smaller one, bound with brown leather and bearing the name of the bank.

"Keep this in a safe place," he said, handing it to her. He withdrew a folded notebook from his pocket and passed it across to her.

Then he rose. "One of these days, I suppose, you'll want to get married?"

She shook her head with a laugh.

"You will," he insisted with a flash of humour; "at some time in her life every girl shakes her head as you did, and they all go the same way."

A little nod, a quick nervous sweep of the hand, and he was leaving the room when she remembered something.

"Uncle," she said, "you have not told me the name of the man whom I must see."

He stopped, hesitating, with the doorknob in his hand.

"It's a man named Comstock Bell," he said; "I will tell you about him later."

The next instant he was gone. She watched him as with quick steps he passed down the road out of sight.

What did he mean by his past life? She was old enough now to know that these changes of name which had once amused her had a serious importance; men are not Schmidt in Berlin one week and Von Grafheim in Prague the next, unless there is something sinister in their profession. She almost wished she had persuaded him to speak out and tell her everything.

She looked at her watch. She had an appointment at six o'clock. She wondered what sort of a man this Mr Cornelius Helder was; it was rather strange that he should have asked her to go to Curzon Street, that he could not find time to interview her at his office. But she was ready to find excuses for any busy man, and the fact did not trouble her greatly.

Helder occupied at floor at 406 Curzon Street. The house was the property of a retired butler who found pleasure and profit in turning the establishment into a high-class boarding-house. Perhaps, "boarding-house" is not the term, since none of the residents had any other meals than breakfast and an occasional supper in their rooms. As it was, even the rent was stiff enough for any man other than one who was in receipt of a very comfortable income, but this Helder was credited with possessing.

Verity Maple was shown straight up to his sitting-room and found him sitting before a large desk smothered with printers' proofs and magazines.

He looked at her keenly as she entered, and rose, offering his hand.

"Take a seat, Miss-er − " His hesitation was artistic; he knew well enough what name she bore.

"I am sorry to bring you down here, Miss Maple," he said when she had told him her name, "but I am such a busy man I had a number of engagements in the city which made it impossible for me to see you."

His tone was brief and business-like, and the unpleasant impression which she had received when she first saw him was to some extent dissipated.

"The work I want you to do," he continued, "is fairly interesting; you speak French, do you not?"

"Yes," she said, and he nodded.

"I am associated with a little journal in which I shall ask you to take an interest," he went on. "It is a journal which is not very well known."

This time his friendly smile was less business-like, and instinctively she resented it. They discussed for a little time the question of salary; he was willing, nay eager, to give her all she asked, another bad sign from her point of view. Just as soon as she could finish the purely business side of the conversation she rose.

"I shall expect you tomorrow," he said.

He held her hand a little longer than was necessary, saw her to the door and into the street. Verity Maple came away from her first interview with her new employer with an undefinable sense of misgiving as to her wisdom in accepting the position.

Any man who knew Helder could have told her things which would perhaps have altered her whole plans entirely, but the only man who knew her well enough to impart that information was Wentworth Gold, who in one swift appraising glance had marked her down as one who was quite capable of taking care of herself. Moreover, he was anxious to learn more of Helder than he already knew, and Verity Maple was the type of girl who could supply that information.

She was halfway down Curzon Street when she heard her name called softly. She turned; Helder was walking behind her, he was out of breath, being one of the men who take little or no exercise. Something of the dismay she felt must have crept into her face, and Helder was annoyed. Like all men of his class and possessed of his idiosyncrasies, he was an immensely vain man; and when he spoke to her now, there was a gruff note in this voice and a hauteur which Verity much preferred to the soft, caressing tone he had used at parting.

"I'm going to Oxford Street," he said brusquely; "are you walking my way?"

She would have liked to have said that she was not, and indeed she would have spoken with truth, but she was anxious to make amends for her unintentional rudeness, and they walked on side by side.

His ruffled feelings were easily smoothed, apparently; he told her he was going to a firm of motor-boat builders, and he spoke in a lordly way of the magnificence of a new craft he was purchasing. It was evidently to be something wonderful in the line of motor-boats, and the cost, which he let fall carelessly, was staggering to a girl who thought in shillings.

He was inclined to talk about money, big money; sums which were almost beyond her comprehension. He outlined schemes in which he was interested, although he gave the vaguest details.

She left him in Oxford Steet and breathed a little sigh of relief when she found her somewhat embarrassing employer had accepted his *congé* with good grace.

Helder was impressed by the girl's beauty; he had never expected anything so rare in colouring, so refined in feature. She would serve two purposes, he thought; that she would serve a purpose which would eventually upset his plans or bring about a drastic change in his life he did not imagine. He made the mistake which many another man has made, of recognizing only the side view of factors.

He watched her until she was lost in the throng which crowded the side streets at that hour in the evening, then he hailed a taxi-cab and drove to his club.

Verity continued her way eastward; she had a little shopping to do which took her longer than she anticipated, for she found on arriving at Victoria that her train had gone. The service was very frequent, however, and she had not long to wait.

She strolled to the bookstall and was idly examining the titles of the new novels, when a man brushed against her. He turned quickly on his heel, and raised his hat with an apology, the stooped to pick up the parcel which in the collision had been knocked out of her hand.

She saw a tall good-looking young man with rather sad eyes; he saw a girl so strikingly beautiful that for a moment he was speechless.

"I'm awfully sorry," he said, as he handed back the parcel with a little smile.

There the matter ended, for raising his hat the young man strode away.

It was Verity Maple's first introduction to Comstock Bell.

She went into the restaurant to get a cup of tea to beguile away the moments of waiting, and to her annoyance found that the second train had gone. She looked at her watch; there was no especial reason why she should go back to Peckham early, and she strolled to Marble Arch and spent a profitable hour in the cinema show.

It was nine o'clock when she got to Peckham; the sky was overcast and it was raining dismally. At the corner of the Crystal Palace Road she noticed a man standing under a lamp on the opposite side of the thoroughfare; she did not see his face – nor for the matter of fact did he see hers – and his back was turned to her.

She reached the house and was inserting the key in the lock when she heard voices. It was not usual for her uncle to have visitors at any hour of the day, and she drew back hesitatingly. The voices were raised; and it seemed that one, peculiarly harsh, was threatening her uncle.

Before the house was a little garden, in which grew three bushy clumps of laurel. As she heard the door click she slipped back out of sight. There was no reason why she should do so, but somehow she felt strangely reluctant to intrude her presence.

The door opened and her uncle came out, bareheaded. With him were two men, one thick-set and sturdy, one tall. The shorter man was smoking a cigar and spoke with an accent which betrayed his American origin.

"You understand," he said menacingly.

Maple replied in a low voice.

"That's all right," said the other with brutal carelessness; "I don't suppose anybody in this street cares two cents what you've done or who you are. We want you to be a good boy," he went on, heavily jocular; "it's up to you to undo any mischief you've already done. He knows" – he jerked his head in the direction of the Rye.

"Why doesn't he come himself?" muttered Maple sullenly.

The other laughed.

"Because he doesn't want to appear in this. Besides, you don't live alone, do you?"

The girl listened wonderingly. Her uncle made no reply to the last remark.

"You'll have something to explain away," said the thickset man, "if you come up against us again."

There was no mistaking the menace in his voice.

"We're out for a big business," he went on, "and not one man or twenty men are going to stand between us and success. Dy'e hear?"

Tom Maple nodded; for a moment there was a pause; then the other man asked suddenly: "Where is he?"

"He is waiting at the end of the block."

For some reason or other his taller companion took no part in the conversation. It struck Verity that he was a foreigner and that he did not very well understand the language, and this, as it turned out, was a shrewd surmise.

"Would you like to walk down and see him?" suggested the short man.

Tom Maple shook his head.

"No," he said. "I know he's there all right," he added, with a note of bitterness in his tone.

With no other word they parted. Tom Maple watched the men go through the gate, then turned and re-entered the house, closing the door behind him.

The girl was worried. What did it mean, what power had these men over her uncle? Who was the mysterious "he" who could not come to the house because she lived there? She hesitated a moment then went swiftly through the gate and followed the two men. They had not gone far and were walking slowly. As they reached the end of the road the man who stood under the lamp crossed to meet them.

They stood talking in low tones. As Verity passed them the third man turned his head slightly, and with a gasp she recognised him.

It was Helder.

She walked on swiftly, hoping that the recognition had not been mutual. She gave a swift glance round as she reached the end of the road and saw they were coming on behind. She quickened her pace, crossed the road, turning up toward Forest Hill. To her relief she saw they made no attempt to follow her, but struck off in the other direction. She waited till they were out of sight, then retraced her steps to the house.

Her uncle was in the kitchen before his table. He greeted her with a nervous little smile when she entered. His lips were trembling slightly, and his hand moved more frequently to his mouth than was usual in his moments of sobriety.

She deemed it advisable to make no reference to the scene she had witnessed, but busied herself with the preparation of supper. He did not move, she noticed; sitting with his hands clasped on the stained deal before him, he stared with unseeing eyes at the wall before him.

When she came in bringing the tray, he looked up quickly.

"Verity," he said. "I'm going to do it, whatever happens."

She waited for him to say something more; she knew he was on the verge of revelation.

"They think they have a lever," he muttered, half to himself; "they think they can push me into doing what they wish, but they have got something to learn – they've got something to learn!"

Throughout the meal she was silent; when at last she rose to leave the little room he looked at her queerly.

"Don't forget that man I told you about," he said, turning with his hand on the door.

"Comstock Bell?" she said.

"Comstock Bell," he repeated.

A MESSAGE TO MR HELDER

Cornelius Helder was a contradiction, and Gold did not like contradictions. "A man is either one thing or the other," was a favourite saying of his; "my experience of life is that he is generally the other."

By Gold's exact measure it was impossible to reconcile the *bon garçon*, a man full of the joy of life, a lover of good living, good stories and luxurious tastes, with the revolutionary preaching red riot and rebellion to those effete and degenerate monarchies which sway Europe.

"It may be affectation, your Excellency," said Gold; "a pose – some men are fond of poses."

He was in the American Ambassador's private study.

"I should hardly describe Mr Helder as young," said his Excellency dryly; "he is passing into the vinegar stage of his salad days."

Gold smiled. He held in his hand a paper, a little eight-paged journal, half of which was printed in foreign characters. The title of this publication was *The Red Monitor*, and Helder made no secret of the fact that he was the financial support, prop, and stay of the little production.

"I must confess," said his Excellency, "I am getting a trifle weary of the cranks our beloved country sends us, and I never expected that a man like Helder, who I should describe as a 'comfortable' man, would run in the direction of anarchism."

"There does not seem to be anything particularly outrageous in this number," Gold said.

"There's not been in any, so far," said his Excellency.

Gold was skimming through the leading article, which was printed in Russian, in characters which suggested that some mischievous boy had been busy turning the letters inside out.

"That is the senselessness of it," said the Ambassador irritably; "this journal is supposed to be secretly distributed amongst the Russian peasantry. Helder might as well spend his money distributing special editions of Walt Whitman's poems."

Gold waited for the Ambassador to explain the reason for the urgent summons he had received. He had read this little journal month by month, since it had made its first appearance two years before; its existence was as well known as the existence of *The Times* or the *New York American*.

They talked for a little while in general terms, then Gold, seeing the Ambassador was getting no nearer to the explanation, asked bluntly:

"What is there about this particular issue of the *Monitor* which annoys you?"

His Excellency rubbed his hands slowly together and leant back in his padded chair.

"You know Helder," he said. "He was telling me the other night at the Terriers' reception that you were the one American in London he had any respect for or confidence in."

A little smile played round the corner of Gold's mouth.

"I mistrust Helder," he said, "when he slops over."

"That may be," said the Ambassador carelessly; "but I want you to put to the test this regard he has for your opinion and judgement. Ask him to give up publishing this journal. The British Government does not like it. Why, he has imported a little colony of Russians somewhere down in a quiet and inoffensive Shropshire village to the scandal of the squire and local clergy." He smiled a little. "He is producing his innocuous rag with all the pomp and circumstance which attend the preparation of a *coup d'état*. The Foreign Office people are very touchy on the matter; they expect him to suddenly blossom forth with suggestions for wholesale slaughter. If he does, of course they will show no mercy; you know that the editor of the Italian paper who suggested the murder of his king was jailed for two years, and I don't want anything like that to happen to a man of Helder's position."

"I will see what I can do," said Gold.

He drove straight to the Terriers from Park Lane. Helder had not arrived. He saw Comstock Bell lunching at a table in the window by himself, and crossing over took a seat on the opposite side.

The young man looked ill, and his right hand was bandaged.

"Hullo!" said Gold, "what's happened?"

"Nothing," said the other shortly, "I caught my hand in a door and I think I have broken one of the fingers."

"I am sorry to hear that," said the other.

"It is not worth while worrying about," said Bell; "it is a bore eating with one's left hand, and I have to use a typewriter for letters – but what of you?"

"What of me?" repeated Gold.

"Are you so used to being shot at by strange gentlemen in the park that you forget all about such trifles?"

Gold smiled grimly.

"I remember all right," he said. He did not pursue the subject, but talked of general matters. At the end of the meal, when the men were taking their coffee, he returned to it.

"See here, Comstock, my boy," he said, "I am going to put all my straights and flushes on the table for you to inspect, and my gone-wrong flushes too. That man who met me last night was out for blood."

"You surprise me," said Bell ironically; "I thought he came to command you to Buckingham Palace."

"Quit fooling," said Gold seriously, "it affects you as well as me. I had a letter asking me to meet one of my men in the Mall last night. Sometimes," he dropped his voice, "it is essential that I should know what certain people are doing; that is my business. My man told me that he would be between the third and fourth electric standards in the Mall. He must have been watched *quis custodiet ipsos custodes*, eh?

Whoever it was followed him to the post. Two men representing themselves as English detectives arrested him for loitering with intent, and my man, a perfectly law-abiding citizen, not wishing for trouble, accompanied his captors. They took him through two parks, bundled him into a cab and marooned him in the wilds of Hampstead Heath."

He chuckled.

"That was smart," he said; "they left a gentleman behind to settle accounts with me – "

"Your friend," repeated the other. "You'll excuse me."

Out of the corner of his eye he had seen Helder standing for a moment in the doorway of the dining-room.

"Is that a friend of yours, too?"

There was a studied carelessness in Comstock Bell's voice.

"No – he's a subject for my insatiable curiosity," answered Gold. With a nod to his companion he crossed the room and passed into the smoke-room beyond.

Helder was turning the leaves of an illustrated paper.

He looked up as the other man came to him.

"I want to see you, my anarchist friend," said Gold. Helder laughed.

"Am I to be deported?" he asked, and made room for the other on the settee by his side; "or am I in danger of a charge of high treason?"

"Nothing quite so heroic," said Gold dryly; "you're in some danger of being a nuisance. I happened to meet the Ambassador the other day, and knowing that I exercise some influence on my young and innocent compatriots, he asked me to make it clear to you that just so long as you continued on your sinful path, it would embarrass him less if you did not look forward with too much eagerness to invitations to the Embassy."

A dull red glow spread over Helder's face, beginning at the bald forehead and descending like a curtain over his cheek.

"You are the little express messenger of the great democrat?" he sneered. "I'd like to get my *congé* from the Embassy first hand, I guess."

It was the first time he had shown himself in this light, an Gold was intensely interested. This was a new Helder and an ugly one. The humour had gone from his eyes, this soft lines about the mouth stretched tight and hard. A curious contradiction, said Gold to himself.

Helder had laboured hard to reach his present position in society. His father had left his artist son a bare income – little more than was sufficient to keep body and soul together. He had had to drop his silver-point work and his etchings, and leave Paris. For years he had worked in London. He dealt in American stock, was reported to have amassed a small fortune when Southern Pacifics boomed sky-high. And he had never looked back.

It had been a fight, but the greater fight had been to establish himself a member of the select little coterie of London's Americans of which Comstock Bell was the bright particular star. Helder was not popular with men, socially he had to win out. There were stories about him which women did not like, a damning circumstance for a man desirous of treading that path to eminence which runs through the drawing-rooms of Belgravia and ends at the Ambassador's dinner-table.

And now he had "got there" he was threatened with social extinction. To the society of the other cranks, to be relegated to the congregation of the "nearly theres."

His eyes narrowed as he looked down at Gold.

"I claim the privilege of my citizenship," he said, "which is my right to do as I please, to order my life in any way which is in the bounds of decency and the law. There is nothing in the *Monitor* which is offensive."

"There is no reason for its existence," said Gold.

"Your cynicism is offensive, Gold."

Cornelius Helder rose to his feet.

"I don't think we need to go on with his conversation."

Gold nodded. "It is pretty unprofitable," he said. "Now – by Jove!" He looked at the clock and began searching his pockets.

"I promised myself to mail a nephew of mine in New Jersey a birthday present."

He drew out his pocket-book and opened it. What he sought was not there.

"Have you any money?" he asked. "American money. I want twenty dollars."

Comstock Bell had come into the room, and Gold's last words were addressed to the world at large.

Helder shook his head.

"Twenty dollars?"

Bell broke in on the conversation.

"I have some money," he said. He slipped his hand into his hip pocket and produced a wallet.

This he opened and extracted the money required.

He handed the bills to Gold, and the third man watched them narrowly.

He saw Gold count the English equivalent into the other's palm; saw him looking at the bills carelessly, then:

"Good God!" said Gold, and Cornelius Helder saw his face go bleak.

COMSTOCK BELL MAKES READY

Gold stared at the young man for fully a minute.

"What is the matter?" asked Bell.

"Nothing," said the other shortly.

With no other word he turned and left the room.

Comstock Bell stood looking after the retreating figure, a puzzled frown on his face.

"What was wrong?" he asked Helder curtly.

His attitude toward the other was always one of polite indifference; under other circumstances, he might not have troubled to ask.

"I know no more than you, Mr Bell," said Helder.

"I don't think Gold can be well today; he has been ragging me about my anarchism."

He smiled ingratiatingly, inviting further conversation.

Bell ignored the invitation.

"Why did you tell him," he asked, "that you had no American money?"

Before lunch he had met Helder and a little discussion arose as to the drawing of Washington's head on a five-dollar bill. They had compared one note with another and Helder had carried Comstock Bell's bills to the window to examine them.

"Did I?" drawled Helder. "I had forgotten I had them; besides," he said, "I am not always out to humour old man Gold."

Bell made no response, and was going away with a little nod when Helder called him back.

"I say, Mr Bell, I wanted to ask you something. Do you know a man named Willetts?"

"No," replied Bell shortly.

"You've never heard of him, eh?"

"Can't say I have: why?"

Helder shrugged his shoulders.

"Oh, it is nothing," he said, "but if you'd spare the time I'd like to have a little talk with you."

"About this man?" asked Bell sharply.

"Yes, and other things."

Comstock Bell hesitated.

"I will call at your office one day this week," he said. There was a note of resolution in his voice.

He passed out of the club, crossed Pall Mall, and strolled aimlessly through the park.

It was a bright spring day; the trees were all glorious, while tender green daffodils and crocuses starred the grass and swayed rhythmically to the breeze. It was a day when men's hearts grew joyful from the very joy of life, when new aspirations sprung in each heart, new and splendid fancies filled the mind. But the stimulation of spring woke no response in Bell's heart. He had made a plan, a terrible plan, he told himself, but he was going through with it, whoever suffered – and he would not suffer least. He would end this terror which weighted his soul.

It was a plan complete in every detail: he had left nothing to chance. Day after day in the silence of his study he had worked out the scheme, jotting down the details and burning the papers so soon as they had taken definite shape and he had committed them to memory.

"Whoever suffered," he repeated and winced.

He reached the Victoria Memorial and crossed the road, continuing his stroll along Constitutional Hill. There was one thing necessary, one link in the otherwise perfect scheme to be discovered. He must have a partner in this matter. He would reward him well.

He had thought of Gold, only to discard that idea, for he knew instinctively that it could not be.

He attracted some attention as he walked. His damaged hand was in a black sling. He smiled as he detected more than one pitying glance in his direction. He smiled, but he was annoyed – annoyed with Helder, more annoyed with himself.

The success of everything depended upon the partner. He had turned over every possible man in his mind. He had a host of friends, but would they stand that test? He thought not.

Helder? Bell had a shrewd idea as to Helder's probity. He thought that Helder would do anything for money; he might do too much. He would sell himself, but then he would sell the man who trusted him. Helder was impossible.

So full was he of his own concerns that he had forgotten Gold, his startled exclamation, and his unceremonious exit. What worried the little man? he wondered.

He was still idly debating Gold's curious attitude when the man he was thinking about hailed him from a taxi-cab. Gold leapt from the taxi, paid the driver, and crossed the road to him.

"I followed you from the club," he said; "I wanted to talk with you."

"Everybody seems to want to talk with me," said Bell good-humouredly; "I was thinking of you when you came up."

"Where can we go?" asked Gold.

"Let us go into the park."

They left the path, and began to walk across the stretch of greensward.

"I am going to be straight with you," said Gold. "I have no doubt you were wondering what upset me, and why I left."

"I did wonder a little," said Bell.

"Well, you needn't worry abut it, because I wanted to call up somebody on the phone to confirm my suspicion. That suspicion has been confirmed."

"What do you mean?" asked Bell.

He stopped in his stride and looked at the other.

"Two of those five-dollar notes you handed to me were forgeries."

"Forgeries!"

"They were forged," repeated Gold. "They were two of many thousands which are now in circulation. Where did you get them?"

"I changed them for a man, a man I met at the *Savoy*, who had arrived from America and had no English money. He wanted a five-pound note for something; he was a member of the party with which I was dining, and I changed it."

Gold's eyes searched his face.

"Is that true?"

"What do you mean?" asked the other with growing resentment in his tone; "why should I tell you a lie?"

"Who was the man?"

At that moment it dawned upon Comstock Bell how the notes came into his possession. He had got them from Helder. Helder, on the pretext of comparing the printing, had substituted the forged notes; but even as he realized this, another idea came to him. Here was an opportunity. It strengthened his plan.

"What was the man's name?" asked Gold.

"A man named Willetts," said Comstock Bell slowly.

"Willetts? You told me last night you had never met Willetts."

"I did not associate the person of whom you spoke with the man I met at the *Savoy*," he said.

Gold shook his head.

"That was all I wanted to know," he said. "I am going to find this Willetts. I have an idea that when I find him I shall be ridding myself of a great deal of trouble."

"You will be ridding me of more," said Comstock Bell.

He was speaking half to himself, and there was no doubt of the sincerity in his voice.

Gold lost no time. Leaving Bell to finish his stroll, he walked quickly to the Piccadilly entrance of the park and found a taxi-cab. He gave his directions and stepped in. In twenty minutes he was in the heart of the City of London.

He dismissed the cab in Threadneedle Street, and came at last through numerous courts and alleys to Little Painter Street. It was a street of old houses, now used as offices, and on one of the doors he found a name painted: "Harold S Willetts, Broker."

He climbed to the third floor, the door of the back room bore the same inscription. He knocked; but there was no answer. He tried the door; it was locked. He shook it gently, but there was no response.

He descended the stairs again. The housekeeper lived in the basement and Gold sought information from him. "No," said the housekeeper, "Mr Willetts was not in."

"When do you expect him?"

The housekeeper was not communicative. Many years' experience in offices had taught him that absent tenants when eagerly inquired for had no desire to have their plans revealed to strangers.

"Well, sir," he said vaguely, "I don't expect him till I see him."

Gold put his hand in his pocket and produced a pound note.

"I know I am bothering you," he said pleasantly, "and wasting your time, but it is necessary that I should know where Mr Willetts is, because I am most anxious to see him."

The housekeeper accepted the note with an apology for the hard times which made it necessary. Under the genial influence of this unexpected wealth he unlocked the secret cupboard of his mind which was labelled "Willetts."

If the truth were to be told, there was little he could tell which was worth half or a quarter of a fraction of the sum.

"He's a gent I have never seen, except in the dark," he said. "He don't do much work here, he merely has his letters sent here."

"How long has he had the office?"

"Two years or more," said the housekeeper; "he spends most of his time in the country or in America."

"Is he American?" asked Gold sharply.

"That I cannot tell, sir," said the other. "All I know is that he pays his rent regularly and that he has got an office. If you would like to see his office, I will show it to you."

It was a plain little room, very simply furnished. A locked roll-top desk, an easy chair, together with a big financial work of reference, comprised the furniture of the room.

Gold took down one of the books from the shelf. It was a Stock Exchange Year-Book of two years previous. He opened it; it was evident from the stiffness of the cover and virgin whiteness of the pages that its owner had little need or excuse to examine its contents. It was the same with the other books.

"That's a curious desk," said Gold pleasantly.

The housekeeper, who was not an imaginative man, saw only a very commonplace roll-top desk, such as might be found, and were to be found by him, in other offices. But twenty shillings makes one polite, and he agreed that it was a curious desk, though for the life of him he could not see anything in it that was not conventional.

"A very curious desk," said Gold. "I've got a desk like it. They are bad desks for a businessman to have," he said in that confidential tone of his which had first interested and eventually undone so many clever men.

"Why, are they dangerous?" asked the man curiously.

"I will show you," said Gold. He took a bunch of keys from his pocket, selected one and inserted it in the lock. He turned it to the left and to the right; with a sharp click the lock went back.

"You see, anybody can open them," said Gold, and to prove his assertion he let the cover roll up. There was nothing on the table save a blotting pad, a bottle of ink and a pen, the nib of which was new and had never been used.

"Anther disadvantage," Gold continued conversationally, "is that if you pull out this drawer and that and the other on the right" – as he spoke he suited the action to the words – "you can't pull the others out."

Now the curious workings of roll-top desks in such little matters as might provide subject for conversation in the private bar of nights were of immense interest to the caretaker. He tried the drawer on the left side. It came out readily enough.

"I think you are wrong sir," he said with a triumphant smile, as though his cleverness were responsible for the other man's mistake. He tried another drawer; that also came out – and the third. There was no difficulty.

Gold was abashed.

"Well, it happens in some cases," he confessed. "In this particular instance I am wrong."

He closed the drawers and pulled down the desk top. There had been no papers of any kind in any of the drawers. He knew now all he wanted to know. There was not the slightest evidence of Mr Willetts' business. Willetts' office was a blind. Whatever his profession was – and Gold made a good guess – he did not pursue it on these premises.

"How often does he come here?" he asked, as he went down the stairs.

"Once a month, at least."

"Any particular day?"

"No, sir, you cannot be sure when he'll come."

"What sort of man is he?"

"Well, as far as I can tell, he is a dark chap with a little stoop."

"Tall?"

"No, sir; I should say he's about middle height; that's how he has impressed me when I've met him on the stairs."

"And his voice?"

"Well, sir, I am rather glad you reminded me of that: he has a foreign accent, more like a Frenchman than an Englishman in his way of speaking."

"And you have no idea of where I can find him?"

"Not the slightest, sir."

"If he comes, you might tell him I called."

"What name shall I give, sir?"

"Comstock Bell," said Gold.

A look of suspicion came into the man's face.

"You are not Mr Comstock Bell," he said.

Gold smiled. "I should have said *from* Mr Comstock Bell," he said carefully. "But how do you know I am not Mr Bell?"

"Because Mr Bell called here himself to see Mr Willetts only two days ago," said the housekeeper.

COMSTOCK BELL CHANGES HIS MIND

Comstock Bell occupied a house in Cadogan Square.

The sombreness of the furniture, which he had purchased with the house was relieved by the beauty of the pictures which adorned his room. If he had a fad, it was represented by an extreme distaste for the conventions of collections.

There was no old master in his house, other than a Virgin of Riberia Espanoleto filched from a Spanish altar, and its main charm, as Comstock Bell would say, lay in its dubious authenticity. But with beautiful examples of the modern school his house was filled, for he was an artist at heart, loving the human painter as much as he loved the work of his hands. It was a keynote of his character, one side at any rate. A cynical critic who once viewed his collection said that Bell's epitaph should be, "He was kind to artists." Examples of his own work were to be found on his walls, for in his early youth he had studied under Gallier and in the inconvenient old *atelier* near the Pont Neuf, isolated from artistic Paris, he had acquired a little of his master's genius.

Bell arrived home at six o'clock, and made his way to the study. It was a big room at the back of the house, the one room which he had furnished himself. There were a dozen letters awaiting him. He opened them as best he could with his one hand. They were mainly invitations. In one corner of the room was a brand-new typewriter. It was one of those convenient little machines made for travellers. Its body was of aluminium, and the carriage folded over till it almost lay on the keyboard. He contemplated the instrument abstractedly for a minute, and then rang the bell.

A man-servant appeared.

"I ordered a rubber stamp to be made for me," he said.

"Yes, sir, a little packet has arrived from the stationers," said the man, and disappeared, to return in a few minutes with the package. He opened the parcel and took out a rosewood box secured by two locks. The keys were fastened to the brass handle of the box by a piece of tape.

"Open the box," said Bell.

The man obeyed. Inside was a small rubber stamp and an ink pad. Bell took up the stamp and examined it. It was a facsimile reproduction of his signature; a stamp which, attached to a cheque, would be honoured. He had arranged this much with his bank, though the manager had demurred at the risk.

Bell replaced the stamp, locked the box, and placed the keys in his waistcoat pocket.

The man was retiring, when Bell called him back.

"Parker," he said, "I am leaving England in a few weeks' time, and I wish you to take charge of the house. I have made provision for your wages to be paid regularly, and I have other instructions to give you later."

"Will you be away for long, sir?" asked the man.

Bell hesitated, fingering his moustache absently.

"I may be away for − a few years," he said.

"Indeed, sir."

If Bell had said that he would have been away for the rest of his life, he would have said no more.

Bell walked to the far end of the room and stood gazing out of the window. The man made a movement as if to go.

"Wait a moment, Parker," he said over his shoulder. He stood irresolutely as if he were not sure of himself, like a man hesitating before two roads.

"I am going to be married, Parker," he said.

It was done; and it was not a difficult beginning. Perhaps if he told Parker often enough he would summon courage to tell his own world.

"I am going to be married," he repeated half aloud.

"May I congratulate you, sir, with all respect?" said Parker, a little dolefully.

Comstock turned with a hard little smile.

"You need not worry about your position," he said; "it will make no difference to you. We shall go abroad – my wife and I."

There was a silence.

"If I might be so bold, sir," said Parker, "do I know the lady?"

"You probably do," said Bell, and his lips twitched. "It is as likely that you know her, as it is that I do."

He changed the subject abruptly.

"I am expecting Mrs Granger Collak in an hour; show her in here."

Parker bowed and left him.

Bell walked to the window.

Mrs Granger Collak was in his mind. She was also in the mind of London. A tall, beautiful woman, delicately moulded, with the face of an angel and the morals of a Catherine.

He looked round the room and smiled in spite of his troubled mind. She would turn this house of his inside out. She would tax his enormous income to its fullest extent. Probably she would set herself to Anglicize him with the object of securing a title for him. People would laugh behind his back and pity him, but no breath of scandal would reach the fragile little woman in New England whom he called Mother. She would accept Grace Granger – would be a little shocked with her perhaps. But there are worse shocks than the presentation of a smart wife.

And Mrs Granger Collak was a clever woman, a discreet woman. She knew how to hold her tongue. The cleverest lawyer at the Bar had discovered that when he cross-examined her in a recent *cause célèbre*.

Comstock Bell made a wry face at the recollection.

She loved travel, and she wanted money, and she was nearly at the end of her tether. She might as well be Mrs Comstock Bell as Mrs Granger Collak. He would only ask her to keep his name out of the mud, and somehow he felt that she would do this.

At six o'clock Parker ushered in the woman whose fate hung in the balance.

She was dressed in a plain tailor-made costume, and her beauty did not suffer, though she was the type of woman who looked her best in dresses of vague line and cloudy substance.

He regarded the tailor-made as a concession to his propriety, and was amused.

"Sit there, won't you?" He pushed a big restful club chair to the side of his desk, so that she faced him.

"Now, what is your trouble?"

"You mean, what is the extent?" she smiled, "I think that if I could raise three thousand pounds, I should be able to get away. I can manage with less," she added, watching his face," and I hate asking you for any."

He opened a drawer in the writing table and took out a cheque-book.

With his uninjured hand he tore out a slip.

"Fill it in," he said, as he pushed it across the table to her. "Make it payable to bearer."

It was then that she noticed the bandaged hand.

"Have you hurt yourself?" she asked in some concern.

"It is nothing," said Bell. He chose a pen for her, then from another drawer he took the rosewood box and opened it. Very carefully he inked the stamp, and when she had blotted the cheque, he pressed the little rubber signature in its place.

"They will cash that for you," he said; "and now I want to talk to you."

She put the cheque in her gold bag, and sat upright in the chair, with her hands folded in her lap.

"Don't prepare yourself for three thousand pounds' worth of advice," he said smilingly. "I do not intend talking to you for your good – but for mine."

He was leaning back in the padded writing chair, his elbows on the arms, his clenched hands under his chin.

"I am thinking of getting married," he said slowly.

"I am glad to hear it," she said with a little laugh; "who is the fortunate woman?"

"I don't know," said Comstock Bell.

She leant forward, a pretty little frown on her face.

"You don't know? My dear Comstock, what nonsense!"

He shook his head.

"It isn't nonsense," he said ruefully. "I am undecided; I was going to ask – "

He stopped. Something within him put a check upon his tongue; a voice stronger than the voice of conscience, more insistent than the voice which urged the expediency of the act, cried "No!"

"Yes?" she asked.

"Oh, somebody!" he said vaguely.

"You don't want to tell me?"

"No – that is it; I don't want to tell you."

Leaning back in her chair she laughed – a bright, delighted little laugh of sheer enjoyment.

"Really, for so terrible a person," she said, "you are a goose. Tell me who she is, Comstock. I know all the women of London. I know them down to the core of their foolish souls. Tell me who she is, and I will tell you if she is worthy of you."

"I don't think I know her," he said, and rose awkwardly.

She shrugged her graceful shoulders and rose, offering him her hand.

"You were going to tell me, and then you were afraid," she said, her eyes dancing. But the laughter died out when she saw his white face. Woman-like, she realized he was suffering.

"I am sorry," she said gently, "and I think I will go. I am very grateful to you, Comstock."

He arrested her thanks with a gesture.

"Don't speak of it," he said. "I will call on you in a day or so; you will not have left town?"

"No, I shall be in London till the end of the week."

He walked with her to the hall door, and opened it for her.

"Goodbye, and thanks," she said.

"Au revoir," said Comstock Bell. "I may call tomorrow, when I may have more courage."

She thought over his words as she drove back to her Knightsbridge flat, and could imagine no reason for his obscurity.

Bell, left alone, settled down to spend the rest of the evening by himself.

He had a little dinner served on a tray in the library, and when this had been cleared away, he locked the library door. Parker, passing the closed portal, heard the slow clicking of a typewriter, the delicate "clack-clack-clack" which marks the operation of the tyro.

At nine o'clock Bell unlocked the library door, and went up to his room. He rang for Parker.

"Where are the rest of the servants?" he asked.

"Thomas is in the servants' hall, sir."

"Tell him to wait there till I ring: I want you to go to Charing Cross and ask what time the night Continental mail arrives."

"I can telephone sir."

"Go, please," said Bell impatiently; "I do not trust telephonic inquiries. If I want Thomas I will ring for him. If I am out when you return, telephone your message to the club, and do not wait up."

He waited until he saw Parker leave the house, then he began to change quickly. From a locked bureau he took a suit of well-worn clothing and put it on. A soft felt hat and raincoat of dark material completed his costume. From a drawer he took a thick packet of banknotes and put them into his pocket. He carefully placed his discarded suit in the wardrobe and locked the door; then, stepping quietly down the stairs, he opened the front door and gained the street.

Whatever indecision he may have displayed that afternoon he showed none now. Avoiding the frequented streets, he made a detour that would bring him to King's Road, Chelsea. He turned into a street that brought him to the river embankment.

It was raining gently. The black river was veiled in a thin mist, through which the green and red lights of a tug, lying broadside on to the river showed faintly.

He walked along till he came to a narrow passage between two wharves. Down this muddy entrance he turned and came at the end to a flight of steps. One gloomy gas lamp projecting from the wall above showed the sullen waters as they pushed and swirled about the steps below.

A little boat was waiting; two men were at the oars in shining oilskins.

"Lauder!" called Bell.

"Ay, ay, sir!" said a voice, and with a touch of the oar the boat was brought to the steps.

"Give me your hand sir; steady!" said the man at the bow.

Bell caught the huge hand extended to him and stepped lightly into the boat; rowing with strong, slow strokes the boatmen pulled for the centre of the river.

"The tide's on the turn," growled one of the men over his shoulder; "that's why the old *Seabreaker*'s all askew."

He indicated the bulk of the tug ahead.

It was a large vessel for its class – a sea-going tug with a high whale deck forecastle, and a breadth of beam suggestive of enormous strength.

The boat came up on the starboard side, and, catching hold of a rope, Bel climbed up the steep rope ladder and swung himself to the tug's deck.

"You must get a proper companion-way, Captain," he said.

The man who had addressed him first, a short, stout man with a big bushy beard streaked with grey, touched his sou'wester.

"I've put it in hand, sir," he said. "It will be fitted at Greenhithe next time I go down the river."

"That had better be tomorrow," said Bell.

He gave a quick look round.

The vessel was a new one, and, for a tug, a model of cleanliness and order. Bulkhead lights illuminated the deck; and aft, where the towing stanchions are usually to be found, the broad well-deck was shut in by glass windscreens and covered to make a cosy state-room. Aft of the chart-room was another and larger cabin, and towards this Comstock Bell made his way, ascending to the tiny bridge to reach it.

The big cabin was divided into two, and was beautifully furnished. The inner cabin was enamelled white. A little brass bedstead stood under one porthole, and an inlaid desk under the other. The floor was covered with a rich Persian carpet, and light came through a cut-glass shade let into the ceiling. The fittings were of silver and a door admitted to a tiny bathroom luxuriously furnished.

Bell made a short survey of the inner cabin, then returned to the outer one. This was as beautifully fitted. One wall was covered with books, bound in dark blue calf. The big settee was soft and the carpet underfoot was as perfect a specimen of the weavers' art as has ever left the looms of Ispahan.

"Come in Captain Lauder," said Bell, for the man waited outside.

Lauder stepped inside.

"Sit down," said Bell. "Now you know your instructions, Captain?"

"Yes, sir."

"You are satisfied with the boat?"

"Quite, sir. I took her out into the North Sea last week, in a stiff sou'wester. She went almost as fast as the Ostend mail packet, and she certainly didn't make as bad weather of it."

"And the crew?"

"Absolutely trustworthy, sir; I've got my own two boys to help me. They've both got mate's tickets. Down below, looking after the engines, I've got my brother George and his son and a young fellow that's courting George's daughter."

"A family party," smiled Bell. "Much depends on you, Lauder."

"You can trust me, sir," said the other quietly. "I haven't forgotten what I owe you. A skipper that has piled up an Atlantic liner on charted rocks doesn't get another ship, even though no lives are lost, and he can prove that the drunkenness of his chief officer was responsible. You've been a good friend to me, sir."

"I owe you something too," said Bell, "especially as I was one of the lives that weren't lost – thanks to your coolness. However, all this is beside the point. When you have fitted your ladder, drop down to Gravesend and wait instructions. Go to your house and stay there till you get my wire, then carry out the instructions I have given you under seal. Remember," he said, "nothing that I ask you to do will be illegal. Neither you nor your crew need worry in the slightest."

"I know that, sir."

"Put this money in your safe." Bell drew a thin roll of notes from his pocket. "It will be sufficient for all expenses and wages for a considerable time."

He pulled on his overcoat and waited whilst the captain resumed his oilskins, then, stepping into the boat, was rowed ashore.

HELDER'S WAY

Helder rang his bell, and the girl, who had been translating an article from *L'Humanité* into English, put down her work reluctantly, and came into his room. Twice that day she had obeyed the summons, and on each occasion his voice had been friendly.

The man was examining the record of a tape machine as she entered.

She waited, with her hands behind her back.

"Oh, Miss Maple!" he said pleasantly; "I called you in to tell you that I am very satisfied with your work."

It was her third day with her new employer, and his approval was singularly repellent to her.

"You can sit down," he said, dropping the tape. "I have got a lot to say to you."

"Thank you, I will stand," she said.

"Please yourself," he said genially. "You don't mind if I sit? Thanks. Now, in the first place, I am going to pay you four pounds a week instead of the three I promised you."

"I think you are paying me as much as I am worth," she replied; "there is very little work to do."

"There will be more," said Helder. "This is my slack season. By the way, you are the niece of quite a famous person, aren't you?"

She flushed.

"I am not being sarcastic," he hastened to add; "you know that Thomas Maple has quite a reputation. Is he not the man who engraved the new Austrian hundred kronen note?"

"I know little of my uncle's business," she replied. "I only know that he was a banknote engraver."

"Was?"

"He has retired now," she said. "But if you do not mind, Mr Helder, I would much rather not discuss him."

He smiled benevolently.

"My dear Miss Maple, don't be offended. A certain fame, and the curiosity that fame arouses, is the penalty of genius."

He looked at the girl. She was more lovely than he had hoped. It was a great stroke getting her into his office – the niece of Tom Maple!

But it was not the material advantage that pleased him. All men, especially clever men, have their weaknesses. A beautiful woman was Helder's. An inflammable man, impulsive in such matters as these, the caution and the discretion which were second nature to him cut loose under the spell of beauty.

"I am going to call you 'Verity,' " he said suddenly.

The girl went red and white.

He walked round to where she stood, numbed by a sudden realization of danger.

She made no movement, staring at him with alarm in her eyes. He placed his hands upon her shoulders and looked down into her eyes.

"Verity," he said again, "we ought to be good friends. I would like you to know all about me."

He looked down into her eyes and she shivered from head to foot. She wanted to thrust him away from her – to run from the room. His touch was hateful – it made her feel ashamed. No man had looked at her, or spoken to her, like that. He had a soft, caressing voice that was loathsome to her, yet she could not leave him. All her will-power had been drawn from her. She felt his arm about her and suddenly found her voice. She uttered a terrified scream and wrenched herself free.

"Hush!" he hissed savagely.

In an instant he had caught her again, and his hand was over her mouth.

His face was livid; he was as terrified as she.

"Be silent," he commanded, "you little fool! You will have all the people in the building in here!"

"Let me go!" she gasped.

He was cursing himself for his folly. He had precipitated the result he had least desired. More, he had lost his grasp of the situation.

He released her, and she staggered back towards the door, her breast rising and falling quickly.

"You will say nothing of this," he said. "I made a fool of myself – and I am sorry."

She shook her head and laid a trembling hand on the doorknob.

"And you will not go home to advertise my folly; do you hear?" He caught her arm again and shook her.

"You'll go back to your work and come again tomorrow as usual. If you don't – " He dropped his face to the level of hers. "If you don't," he breathed, and his big face was demoniacal in its malignity, "by God, I'll find you and kill you! Worse, I'll be about, d'ye hear?" He shook her arm: "I'll say things about you that people will believe. Things that will make you wish you were dead."

"Let me go," she said faintly.

He took her in his arms; she was nearly fainting.

"Give me a kiss," he said savagely, "and tell me you forgive me."

He bent his head towards her. She felt limp and helpless. His lips brushed hers; and she screamed – screamed in an agony of fear and loathing.

"Damn you!" he said, when the door opened to admit Comstock Bell.

Helder released his hold of the girl. His face was as white as hers.

He was shaking. He saw the look of disgust in the other man's eyes and knew that he understood.

"This girl," he said incoherently, "she threw herself at my head, Bell – she did – by God! – I am only human!"

Bell looked from the man to the girl. She stood with her back to the wall, her eyes closed, her face deathly white.

53

EDGAR WALLACE

"Helder," he said, "you're a liar and a fool, too, if you think you could deceive me. You've been behaving like the blackguard that you are, and which everybody knows you are."

The girl opened her eyes and looked at him. For a moment they looked at one another – the tall young man, and the girl dishevelled and fainting.

Then she stumbled forward, and Bell caught her in his arms. He carried her into the outer office and sat her on a chair. She had not fainted, for her eyes opened again and she murmured her thanks. He was looking at her curiously, thoughtfully.

"Take your time," he said gently. "I will keep this man engaged, and when you are ready and feel well enough just to go out and take a taxi home. Have you got enough money?"

She nodded.

He saw that she was on her way to recovery, and re-entered Helder's office. He was sitting at his desk, a picture of sullen rage. Comstock Bell closed the door behind him and looked at him contemptuously.

"What an impossible scoundrel you are," he said. "If I did my duty I should take you by the scruff of the neck and drop you out of the window."

Helder said nothing, only he looked up from under his brows, and unmistakable hatred blazed in his eyes.

Uninvited, Comstock Bell drew up a chair to the other side of the table at which the man sat.

"Whilst I am here," he said, "we might as well discuss the matter which brought me here."

With an effort Helder pulled himself together. Though he knew that Bell was the last man to carry stories, he knew that he had the power to ruin him, and he was anxious to excuse himself for his own satisfaction.

"I daresay you think I have behaved badly?"

"Cut that out," said Bell shortly; "I know you've behaved abominably. I could forgive you anything but the lie you started to tell. I don't want to discuss the matter; let me hear what you have to say about Willetts."

"You may not be anxious to know," said Helder, and curled his lips.

"I am anxious to know anything that affects Willetts," said Comstock Bell steadily.

Helder rose and paced the room. He felt he was getting under control again; it was necessary that he should be master of the situation.

Suddenly he turned.

"Willetts," he said, "was the man who forged a £50 banknote some years ago, and there is a police warrant out for his arrest."

"Yes."

Bell displayed no emotion.

"Moreover, I have reason to know," Helder went on, "that either you passed the notes that Willetts forged, or you were privy to the act."

"Yes?" said Bell again, with a note of interrogation in his voice.

"Furthermore," said Helder, "you have financed Willetts – you have been paying him to keep quiet – and now, for some reason, you contemplate betraying him."

"Who told you this?"

"I found it out by accident," said Helder. "I got proof of it last night."

"What is your proof?"

"You came into the Terriers' last night, did you not?"

"Yes, I was there for a time," said Bell quietly.

"You wrote a letter in spite of your injured hand. Your injured hand is only a ruse to explain to your satisfaction, or to somebody else's, the disguised hand in which you wrote."

He unlocked a drawer in this desk and took out a piece of blotting paper. "And you blotted your letter," he said triumphantly. "Shall I tell you what you wrote?"

"You need not trouble," said Bell coldly.

"You wrote to Inspector Morrison of Great Scotland Yard, and your words were these."

He held up the blotting paper to the light.

" 'The name you want in connection with the *Cercle de Crime* forgery is Harold Willetts; he is now carrying on business as a stockbroker in Little Painter Street, EC. You will find he returns to town in eight days' time, and you will discover sufficient evidence in his office and on his person to convict him of his crime.' "

He refolded the paper and put it back in the drawer.

"Did you write that?" he asked.

"I may have done."

"I knew a long time ago that you were concerned in it," said Helder. "It was a great stroke of luck that I got this blotting paper. And you," he went on with a snarl, "are the man who comes preaching morality to me and telling me what I may or may not do – a man who, to save himself, betrays another not so well circumstanced as himself; whose disappearance from the world would not create the same stir in society. Bell," he said – he leant forward over the table, and his voice trembled with passion – "I could ruin you, damn you!"

Comstock Bell said nothing for a moment; then he bent forward.

"And I could ruin you," he said, and whispered one word.

One word only, but Cornelius Helder fell back in his chair, staring at the man who held his life and liberty in his power.

Bell took his hat and turned to the door.

"Forgery," he said, carefully brushing his hat on his arm, "seems to be a peculiar habit of people in our set. Some so it for amusement and accumulate years of trouble; some do it cold-bloodedly for profit and acquire a reputation for the possession of commercial qualities."

He chose all his words with great deliberation.

"They tell me you have a little printing establishment in Shropshire. If I were you," he said, "I should close down that business and establish my Russian draughtsmen and my Russian engravers in more unobtrusive surroundings."

WHAT TOM MAPLE FOUND

"John B Wanager, who is the head of the Bill Department of the States Treasury, says there are twenty million dollars' worth of forged bills in circulation. This is the startling news which has created the greatest sensation in Wall Street, and which nearly affects every citizen.

" 'I should say there are twenty million dollars' worth of bills in circulation,' said Wanager to a *News Herald* man. 'The Treasury are considering the advisability of making drastic changes in the appearance of paper currency. These bills are so perfectly forged and printed that it is impossible for any but Treasury officials to detect them. I believe that they are being printed by the cart-load somewhere, and our detective department is satisfied that somewhere is in Europe. The notes are brought over in bulk, and by some means they escape the customs examination. Generally speaking, the forgeries are perpetrated on bills of small value, and the forgers must have the most perfectly organised system of distribution.' "

Wentworth Gold read this cutting in a New York paper, without the distress he would have experienced if he had read it on the day previous. That morning he had had a telegram from Maple – a telegram which had brought joy to his soul – and he was on the way to obey its summons when a cutting letter from the Embassy reached him. The thing was public property now; he had wished to have a solution of the difficulty without unnecessary publicity.

He drove to the little house in Peckham, and was surprised when the door was opened to him by Verity Maple. She looked ill, but he did not know the reason.

"I've found it, Mr Gold."

Maple came up the passage with gesticulating hands and a smile of triumph on his unhealthy face. He was nervously eager to show the detective his discovery.

The kitchen table was in its usual condition of disorder; but there was one phial which Gold had not seen before. It was a little narrow bottle, filled with a colourless liquid. With hands which shook, Maple unfastened the wallet where he kept the experimental notes, and drew out a handful of bills. They had not been employed for experimental purposes, Gold noted. The other uncorked the phial.

"Watch this," he whispered thickly.

He dipped his finger into the liquid, and one by one he took the bills and pressed his damp finger on the left-hand corner. The first one showed no result, except a little wet patch where he had touched it. Nor did the second.

"Good – good notes!" he almost shouted.

With the third it was different. He had hardly moved his finger before the spot where he had touched the bill turned a faint mauve.

"That is the action," he said, "of the chemical upon the watermark." He spoke a little incoherently.

Again he tried with another note, and again there grew slowly to view the little mauve patch.

He went through all the notes, and when he had finished he spread them on the table.

"The mauve is mauve," he said with emphasis.

Gold saw that he had been drinking, but knew that he worked better so.

"Nothing will make, nothing will remove the stain."

He nodded his head wisely. "This is my discovery, Mr Gold. Tonight I will give you the formula of Tom Maple's Liquid Detective." He laughed to himself. "Throughout your wonderful country, in every bank, in every store, Tom Maple in a little bottle will sit waiting to pounce upon the shams and counterfeits."

In a flash Gold realized the importance of the discovery. It was a cumbersome method, but it was effective. No note once branded with its infamy could repass in circulation; this was the test which scientists in Europe and America had been striving to discover.

"Let me have the formula now," said Gold.

"Give me till tonight," said the man, and waved the other off unsteadily; "I want to work it out exactly."

Gold looked at his watch. He would have liked to have waited until the experiment was completed. He was worried – for him. He saw the undoing of this gang of forgers, and fretted at the delay.

"I am going into town," he said, "to see the Ambassador. I shall be back – ?" He paused.

"Nine o'clock," said Maple.

The girl had not been present at the interview. He saw her as he passed into the little drawing-room, sitting by the window, gazing thoughtfully into the prosaic street.

"I am going to talk to your niece for a little while," he said, and went to her.

She looked round as he entered.

"You have left Helder, I hear," he said.

She nodded. "Yes, I have left him."

He waited for her to say something more.

"Was he unsatisfactory?"

She flushed hotly.

"Please don't talk about him," she said.

"H'm!" said Gold. "I am sorry I advised you to go. You did not let me know that you knew him."

He left the house and walked down to Peckham Rye.

His heart was light, and he stepped out with a springy gait as one who knew no trouble. He was obviously more pleased than he usually permitted himself to be. Two men who had followed him, who had watched him into the house and out again, were not so pleased. They kept him in sight, walking on the other side of the road, till he entered the railway station and disappeared.

One man was dark, and wore his hair cut very short; he had the traces of an old wound on his chin, and was apparently a foreigner. The other was English in appearance, though he betrayed his trans-Atlantic origin when he spoke to ask a loafer the way to the nearest telephone.

The two men walked down High Street, and whilst one went to the telephone to speak, the other stood gazing into a shop window. This was all that was seen of them, or, at any rate, noted.

At six o'clock that evening Verity Maple was summoned by a telegram to London. She went, leaving her uncle at work, and came down to Peckham by the same train as Wentworth Gold.

He met her on the platform at Victoria.

"We'll travel together, if you don't mind," he said, "and I shan't talk to you about your employer. I know a great deal more about him than you imagine, and I have been kicking myself that I allowed you to run the risk of annoyance."

"I seem fated to be annoyed," she said with a little smile. She had recovered much of her spirit and some of her colour.

He found a carriage for her, and they got in.

"What's been annoying you now?" he asked.

For answer she took a telegram from her handbag and handed it to him.

"I must see you at once," it ran, and was signed by a name which was not familiar to Gold.

"Who's it from?"

"It was from one of the executors of Lord Dellborough," she said, "and naturally I thought they wanted some information from me which I was able to give – I was his secretary, you know – and I have been to Hampstead on a wild-goose chase."

"Why?"

She folded the telegram up and put it in her bag.

"For a very good reason – I was not sent for," she said. "The telegram was a hoax."

"A hoax?" asked Gold, and felt a sinking at heart.

Somebody, for some reason, desired her absence from the house. He sprang out of the train as soon as it pulled into the station, and ran down the stairs.

There was a taxi-cab in the station yard, and he hailed it.

"Drive to Crystal Palace Road," he said, and gave the number, "and drive as fast as you can."

The girl saw nothing more in this than his anxiety to save time.

"You in a great hurry," she said laughingly, and stole a glance at his face. What she saw frightened her.

"What is it?" she asked anxiously.

"Oh, nothing – I hope," he said.

The cab stopped with a jerk outside the house, and Gold jumped out.

"Wait here!" he said. He gave her no reason, but she obeyed, and stood by the gate. He knocked at the door, and there was no response.

"I have a key," she said.

"Give it to me." He took the key from her hand and opened the door. She noticed that he closed it behind him. She did not see him slip a revolver from his hip pocket.

"Maple!" he called again.

He walked along the passage and pushed at the kitchen door. There was something heavy behind it – something heavy but yielding. He put his shoulder to the door; it gave way and fell over with a little thud.

It was dark in the kitchen and he struck a match.

On the floor in a huddled heap lay Maple, muttering to himself in a drunken stupor. An empty whisky bottle explained everything.

Gold sprang to the table and searched it eagerly.

There was no sigh of the phial. The notes he had been experimenting upon had disappeared.

The detective looked down at the man at his feet and cursed him savagely.

He tried to rouse him, but to no purpose, and went out to the troubled girl.

"Your uncle is not well," he explained; "have you any friends to whom I could take you?"

There was no need to ask what was the nature of her uncle's illness. She saw Gold's anger and understood it.

"I – I think I will go back to town," she faltered. "I have some friends – "

He nodded, closed the door, and accompanied her. Maple would keep. The providence which exercises a special care of the drunkard would take care of him.

He saw the girl to the station and put her in a train. Then he returned to the house.

As his cab turned into Crystal Palace Road another cab passed him, driving swiftly in the opposite direction.

He reached the house and entered, closing the door.

Walking down the passage he kicked something with his foot and stooped to pick it up. It was a fine steel tool such as engravers use.

This he slipped into his pocket and made his way to the kitchen. The apartment was empty. Tom Maple had gone.

WILLETTS WRITES A LETTER

At nine o'clock one night, when the stray light of day still lingered in the skies, as though loath to afford the jaded Londoner respite from toil, a tall man came into the office in Little Painter Street. The building had been closed for the night, but he opened the front door with a key, stepped into the passage, and closed the door behind him. He listened for a while to assure himself that the offices were untenanted. He knew that at that hour the caretaker would probably have gone.

After a minute's hesitation he walked quickly upstairs till he came to the door marked Willetts. This he opened and entered.

He threw up the desk, took a sheet of paper from a drawer at the side and began writing, first switching on the light which overhung the desk. He wrote steadily for the greater part of an hour. Once he stopped to take a cigarette from a case. He was careful to flick the ash into the waste-paper basket, careful even to the point, when it had burnt itself down to within an inch of his lips, to open the window and throw out the end into the paved court below.

It was remarkable that he did not attempt to blot any of the sheets. He spread them out flat on the top of the desk and allowed them to dry.

When he had finished, he gathered all the pages together and read them over carefully. Then he took from his case a leather pocket-case, took out three American bills, each to the value of a thousand dollars, placed them inside a long envelope, and carefully addressed them.

He put the envelope into his pocket. He switched out the light and sat, his hands thrust into his pockets, his head sunk on his breast, before the open desk. He heard a city clock strike eleven, and then he rose with a little sigh. He walked to the windows, opened them to rid the room of any trace of smoke, and then carefully shut them.

He opened the door and listened. The building was in perfect quietness. He had expected the return of the caretaker, but that worthy had been retained at his favourite hostel by an argument on the ever-engrossing subject of compulsory service.

He went down the stairs, through the narrow passage, into the street. At a pillar-box he stopped to post his letter. It was addressed to Comstock Bell at the Terriers' Club. He smiled a little as he posted it.

He reached Broad Street, then turned in the direction of Liverpool Street, and so into the Metropolitan Station, and became absorbed in the stream of passengers which moves east and west all hours of the day and night.

Comstock Bell came to the Terriers' Club to lunch the next day. As luck would have it, he had met Helder on the steps of the club. The porter handed him a letter; it was addressed in a sprawling hand. The expert would have, without hesitation, marked it down as disguised.

Helder was a close observer as Bell turned the envelope over, weighed it in his hand, and glanced abstractedly at the postmark. He ran his little finger under the flap and tore it open. The letter was of five sheets, very closely written, but what attracted Helder's notice were the three notes.

"An unknown benefactor?" he said pleasantly.

Bell glanced quickly through the letter, frowned, and replaced it with the money in its envelope.

"No," he replied shortly.

After lunch he went into the writing-room. Helder followed carelessly, took another seat at a table close by, and commenced a perfectly unnecessary letter. The writing-room was empty save these two.

Helder was intensely curious. It was his business to know as much about Comstock Bell as he could possibly discover. When Bell rose from the table and went out, Helder strolled casually past the place where the other had been sitting in the hope of gleaning some scrap of information to add to his store.

He uttered an exclamation as he came to the table, for there, lying by the blotting pad, was a letter Bell had left.

Helder walked quickly to the window, which looked out upon the street. If Bell had left the club, he would have to pass there in a few seconds. He waited impatiently. By and by he saw the tall figure of the young millionaire walk rapidly past the window where he stood.

He looked round the room. The door was half glass. There was a long corridor leading to the room; from where he stood he could see any possibility of interruption.

After another glance at the window, he stepped to the table, took up the letter and opened it. He stood in the shadow of the curtains, from whence he could command a view of the steps below.

He pulled out the letter and scanned it eagerly. It was in the same sprawling hand which he had noted on the envelope. It was a curious letter – a letter of penitence and of regret. The writer said that he owed Bell everything; he returned, he said, the money which the millionaire had advanced. Quickly Helder turned to the last page. He saw, as he had anticipated, that it was from Willetts. It was an inconsequent letter, almost incoherent. It begged Bell to preserve the secret of the writer's identity, and wound up with a platitude and a reference to Providence which made the reader's lips curl a little contemptuously.

"A squealer, I guess," he said.

Very quickly he refolded the letter, replaced the banknotes, and put it back in the position in which he had found it.

He glanced through the window again. Bell was returning with quick strides: he had missed the letter. Helder had time to leave the room; he was in the vestibule when Bell passed through on his way to the writing-room. Helder waited.

65

The other reappeared, a packet in his hand. Looking neither to left nor right he disappeared again out into the street.

The information that Helder had been able to secure merely confirmed his earlier suspicions. Willetts, the forger for whom the police were searching, was in London, and Comstock Bell had it in his power, if he so willed, to bring about the other's arrest.

Why did he not do so? That was the question which puzzled the American as he drove back to his flat. He knew the history of the forged banknote, because the subject of forgeries interested him intensely, and with good reason. Comstock Bell himself must be under suspicion for the other man's offence; might, indeed, focus all suspicion upon himself but for the providential existence of Willetts. Nobody in London associated the young millionaire with the forged banknote crime. There was no reason why Comstock Bell should not have done at once with the business, the remembrance of which obviously distressed him. Yet here was the man to his hand; he could be arrested with little trouble. Why did he hesitate?

Such an explanation that Comstock Bell held his hand out of pity, out of humanity, out of any of the finer qualities that go to the making of the human soul. Helder did not consider twice. There was no place in his mental arrangements for sentiment. He gave people credit for the worst motives, denied them all benefit of the best.

When he reached his room, he locked the door behind him, opened his desk, and took out a small flat volume. For two hours he was busily coding a message, which he despatched that afternoon to three different addresses.

All accounts of Helder agree that he was a methodical man. He had an extraordinary gift for organization, which lent to his peculiar fault the very elements of success. He was deficient in certain moral traits, but men, judging men, are apt to overlook the worst features of their fellows and palliate any shortcomings with the excuse that the object of criticism is only human.

His work finished, the book replaced, and the door unlocked, he sat down to await a visitor. He glanced at his watch; it was nearly five o'clock, and he rang the bell and ordered tea, for he was an abstemious man and seldom drank wine before dinner.

His visitor came soon after the servant had brought the tray; a sturdy man, clean-shaven, obviously ill at ease in the refinement of Helder's surroundings.

"Sit down, Tiger," said Helder genially.

He waved his hand to a chair facing the light.

The other seated himself carefully, placing his hat beneath the chair.

"Mr Helder," he said – there was a hint of a drawl in his voice – "we've got to get into a new line."

Helder nodded.

"I know," he said, "our men are complaining about the difficulty of changing American notes in Europe. We shall have to cater for the home market."

Tiger Brown nodded vigorously.

"That's so," he said, with a little sigh of relief. "I was real afraid you would not see with me. The American stuff is all right, but our people are getting scared. The Treasury have got all their best men at work, and there's a rumour they have found a new testing method. The man in Philadelphia we usually send five hundred bills a month is only taking a hundred. I think we'd better cut out the American issue and concentrate on the French."

Helder paced up and down the room. He had gone to the door after his visitor's entrance and locked it. Absently he crossed again, lifted the *portière* and tried the door. Tiger Brown's eyes narrowed.

"You're a bit scared yourself, aren't you?" he asked sharply.

"No, no" said Helder quickly, "not exactly nervous – careful, that's all. I agree with you about the American issue; we'll give it a rest. These French notes we sent out – ?"

"NG," said the other curtly. "I don't know why it is, but somehow they don't look good. They don't feel good, and they don't make good. They miss the touch."

"What about that fellow Maple?" he asked after a pause.

Helder pursed his lips.

"I don't know that we could touch him," he said; "he's working for Gold."

"Then you've got no pull?" persisted the other. "Can't you show him a cop?"

The other shook his head.

"You can't show cops in this country," he said grimly. "There's no pull whatever in big matters like these. You can square the cop, but there's a man higher up; you can square him, perhaps; but there's still a man higher up; and the system is such that Scotland Yard can always drop somebody new into the game without anybody knowing. It isn't that the police are the most honest in the world, it's the system that beats you every time."

Again he paced the room slowly.

"Maple," he repeated, half to himself, "I wonder – "

"Could you not bluff him?" persisted Brown. "He's got a daughter – "

"A niece," corrected Helder. "We won't discuss her."

"Say," said Tiger impatiently, "we can't consider nieces and daughters. We've got to make good, and it just doesn't matter how we do it, so long as we do it."

Helder did not reply.

"What about this Mr Gold?" asked his visitor.

"He's the big danger," said the other gravely. "Gold worries me because I don't know exactly what power he had got or what he is working at. He is a difficult proposition – a connecting link between Washington and London."

He paused before Brown, and looked down at him thoughtfully.

"We might get Maple," he said. "He's the best engraver in Europe. Anyway, there's no harm in trying. He wasn't very ready to be bluffed the last time you interviewed him."

"He might be now," said Brown with a smile. "I remember when I was working for Harragon, there were people who could not be bought or bullied the first time or the second time. It was after the third or fourth try on that they began to eat out of our hand."

For another hour they sat discussing plans, and then they left Curzon Street; Brown going first, the other following at five minutes' interval.

They joined one another at Piccadilly Circus – Helder was going east, and the other was accompanying him. They went into the tube station, took their tickets, and entered the lift. There were about a dozen people in the elevator. The attendant closed the door. Suddenly there was a startled exclamation from a lady.

"I've been robbed!" she cried.

Two men of good appearance were standing next to the elevator man. One of them walked forward and spoke to her. He turned blandly to the company.

"This lady has been robbed," he said. "I am Detective-Sergeant Halstead from Scotland Yard. This lady has lost her purse and a pocket-book, and I shall have to ask you gentlemen either to submit to a search or else accompany me to a police station."

The other man stepped up to his side. Helder's first feeling was one of intense annoyance, then of alarm. The other men in the elevator, with the exception of Tiger Brown, submitted calmly to the indignity of a quick search. It was the most superficial of examinations to satisfy the police officers. At the request of the sergeant the lift had been lowered half-way down, that no curious eyes should witness the proceedings.

It came to Helder's turn.

"I absolutely refuse," he said loftily.

The detective turned inquiringly to Tiger Brown.

"You don't search me," said Brown.

"Then I have no course other than to take you into custody," said the detective.

Five minutes later the two men found themselves in a taxi-cab *en route* for Vine Street. On the way to the station Helder cursed his folly. There was no reason why he should not have submitted to a search, except the vague apprehension that there might be upon him some evidence of guilt.

If the examination of the other men in the elevator had been superficial, it was sufficiently thorough in their case. Their pocket-books were examined, and Helder observed with a quickening of his heart that the fifty-dollar bills were submitted to a very keen scrutiny.

"I'm very sorry, gentlemen," said the detective, when the search had been completed and their goods handed back to them. He was large, stout, and urbane, and he smiled genially.

Helder, who was not so genial, gave a brief but bitter opinion of the capacity of the Metropolitan Police.

"You shall hear more of this," he said.

"It's your own fault," said the Inspector, unperturbed. "We have a complaint somebody is robbed – you refuse to submit to a search – what else could we do?"

Helder said nothing. With his companion he walked quickly from the charge-room, down the stone steps. In the middle of the flight he paused, for, smoking a cigar, walking along the edge of the pavement was Wentworth Gold.

He greeted his frowning compatriot with the most innocent of smiles.

"Hello, Helder," he drawled; "I've come too late. They telephoned me they had arrested you, and I was coming along to put matters right."

"You were, were you?" said Helder between his teeth. "Well I have put things right without your assistance, and" – he turned to the other – "you will be interested to learn that they found nothing."

Gold's eyebrows rose.

"What did you expect them to find?" he asked coolly.

Helder did not answer. He turned abruptly on his heel and, followed by his satellite, strode rapidly away.

He saw the whole plot: the faked robbery, the providential detective conveniently at hand to search him.

He shivered a little as he thought that if it had been the day before some banknotes would have been found in his possession.

He knew a young man on the staff of the *Post Journal*. He would take the bold step of telling him the story of the arrest and unjustifiable search. And this he did, sparing no detail. It was a bold move, and one that Gold had not anticipated.

The detective smiled wryly next morning as he read an account of the "Hold up of an American Gentleman. Extraordinary Police Action."

Scotland Yard would not like that. They were very sensitive to anything that reflected upon their discretion and their supreme wisdom. It was only with the greatest reluctance that they had agreed to aid him in his plan, and the next time he needed their assistance there would be difficulties.

He shrugged his shoulders philosophically. He had played for a big stake and he had lost – temporarily, he added to himself.

VERITY RECEIVES A PROPOSAL

Comstock Bell put down the paper he had been reading.

He folded the journal, tucked it away out of sight, and looked at the clock on the mantelpiece. He had no misgivings now. He took up a letter from his table. It was from Mrs Granger Collak, and was dated Naples. He smiled as he thought of the bombshell he might have dropped before her. He heard the distant tinkle of a bell, and a minute later Parker entered.

"Miss Maple," he announced.

Comstock rose to meet her. She looked ethereal in her sorrow.

"I'm obliged to you for coming," he said. "Do you mind if I ask you what are your plans?"

"I have no immediate plans," she said; "Mr Gold has very kindly advanced me some money and has promised that his Government will find my uncle."

"His Government is mine," he smiled.

She looked surprised.

"You think we Americans should wear hayseed beards," he laughed.

"That we should chew tobacco, and say 'I guess' at every sentence."

"As Mr Gold does," she said demurely, and he laughed again.

Then her face clouded.

"It seems dreadful that I can smile," she said, her eyes filling with tears, "so soon after – "

He nodded sympathetically.

"I think I know how you feel," he said, and he walked to the window – a trick of his when he was worried. "I believe your uncle will come back; that the men who are suspected to have carried him off meditated no harm – " He stopped.

She looked up and saw him outlined against the window; caught a glimpse of his fine profile and wondered what the story of a man such as he could be. What interests bound him to life? What did men such as he find in the world – the world which lay at their feet as a ball for kicking?

He was a fine specimen of a man. She had seen that on the day when she met him first; she wondered what woman dominated him – he would be an easy man to rule, she judged – he was so gentle, so kindly, so innately chivalrous.

He came back to her.

"Miss Maple," he said, "have you any other relatives?"

"None," she said.

"Friends?"

She shook her head.

"Save those I am staying with now, I have no friends," she said.

"I was at a convent school in Belgium till I was quite grown up. I hardly knew my uncle till a few years ago."

He nodded, walked to the door, and opened it. She thought it was strange; later she understood the delicacy of the act.

"I am going to say something to you," he said, "which will alarm you; but I want you to believe that I say it with a full sense of my responsibility, and with the deepest respect for yourself."

"Whatever you say, I shall believe that," she said quietly.

He took a turn up and down the room, then stopped suddenly before her.

"Miss Maple, I want you to marry me," he said.

She half rose, and he walked a little way from her.

"Do not be alarmed," he said smilingly, "I have left the door open and my servants are within call."

"But – Mr Bell – " she gasped, a picture of amazement and alarm.

"Wait!" He raised his hand. "You are alone in the world – I also am master of my life. I want you to make a sacrifice: not the sacrifice which women are ordinarily called upon to make. You shall be mistress of – yourself. I offer you a marriage which will mean freedom to you. I do not wish to talk of such things as material advantage, but I could make you one of the richest women in London."

"But I do not love you, nor you me," she said in a low voice, reproach in her sad eyes, "and such a marriage would be an unholy thing – a dreadful crime – which all your wealth could not palliate."

She rose.

"Wait, please."

She sat down again. There was an entreaty, almost agony, in his voice.

She sat in silence while he talked. Halfway through his story she rose and closed the door. He talked now hopefully, now bitterly; till the light in the sky faded and she could only see the black outline of the man as he walked to and fro before the window, his hands nervously gesticulating as he talked.

It was quite dark when he let her out into the street. He came bareheaded to the pavement and handed her into a cab.

"Tomorrow?" he said.

"Tomorrow," she repeated. She gave him her hand and he raised it to his lips.

Gold came in to supper at the Terriers'.

He found a typewritten letter waiting for him, and recognised the characteristic type as Comstock Bell's.

He opened it and read it carefully. Halted halfway down to the drawing-room and read it again. He replaced it carefully in his inside pocket and went in to supper a much-astounded man.

He snatched a hasty meal, for he was a busy man in these times; too busy to talk to Helder, who buttonholed him in the lobby after supper.

"Say, Mr Gold, you're the man I wanted to see."

"And you," said Gold, "are one of the six millions of people in this city I do not wish to speak with – what it is?"

"I think I can tell you something that you want to know," said the other.

Gold heaved a deep sigh.

"You are the hundredth man I've met today, I guess, who wants to tell me something I ought to know; get busy, Helder, for I haven't much time."

Helder bent his head and, lowering his voice, said: "Willetts is to be arrested tomorrow."

The detective looked at him keenly.

"Who told you this – and what do you know of Willetts?"

"Never mind who told me – it is true. And I know Willetts is the head of this gang which is circulating forged bills – the head of the gang which has stolen your friend Maple."

"You know about that, do you?"

There was a curious glitter in Wentworth Gold's eye.

"It is fairly evident," Helder went on. "Willetts is already wanted for forgery. He has an office in the City which is obviously used as a blind to cover his real business. I tell you he is a crook."

"Do you know him?" asked Gold curiously.

"I have seen him," he said, "and I remember him well. He was a student in Paris, and a contemporary of mine."

"Was Comstock Bell a contemporary of yours?" asked Gold.

"Yes, but Bell and Willetts were in the same school. Willetts was a quiet, lanky youth in working hours, but was pretty outrageous at night. He disappeared from Paris after the scandal, and I have never heard of him again until recently."

"And you think he is the man who distributes the notes?"

"I am sure," said Helder eagerly, "and I am as sure that Bell has been behind him."

"That's absurd," said Gold emphatically. "Bell is a man of very large fortune. He might have played the fool as a youngster, but there is no reason in the world why he should be a scoundrel now. How do you know Willetts is to be arrested?"

Helder shook his head, smiling.

"You must find that out," he said. "I know."

A man with a stoop and a slight limp walked slowly across Finsbury Square late that night.

There were very few people about, and the constable on point duty watched him carefully, from sheer *ennui* more than from any desire to faithfully discharge his duty "to take keen and careful observation of all unusual circumstances and people."

The man invited attention from his infirmity. He wore a black Inverness cloak, a broad-brimmed wide-awake hat, and long, black hair, brushed until it bunched behind, suggesting the musician.

He reached Broad Street — at this hour of the evening given over to a few belated pedestrians bound for the railway station — and continued his way towards the Bank.

Had anyone troubled to follow him, they might have wondered why he took so circuitous a route unless it was that he was endeavouring to kill time. As a City church clock struck eleven, he found himself in the broad open space behind the Royal Exchange. A man who had been slowly walking up and down the pavement of Threadneedle Street joined him halfway across the big pavement.

"Ah, Clark," said the man, "you have no letter?"

He spoke in French.

"No, Mr Willetts," said the man. "Have you any work for me?"

His French was the French of the schoolroom, correct in construction, but the pronunciation distinctly English.

The man he called Willetts shook his head.

"Tonight — no," he said.

"There have been people inquiring for you," said Clark, "and I have been questioned as to your whereabouts."

"Oh!" said the other carelessly, "this may often happen. You will tell them that I am abroad. There is nothing more?"

"No, m'sieur."

"Then good night."

With a curt inclination of his head the man in the Inverness parted from his clerk, and went limping in the direction of Cheapside.

Two men followed him. They had no difficulty in keeping him in sight, for the streets were deserted and he walked very slowly.

He had not gone far along Cheapside before a taxi-cab overtook him, and he beckoned it.

One of the shadowers increased his pace and came up as he was giving his directions.

He turned back and spoke quickly to his companion.

"He's going to the American Embassy," he said in a low tone.

Another taxi was hailed.

"Follow that car in front," said the stouter of the two; "don't let it out of your sight."

The taxi driver touched his cap, and followed less than half a dozen yards behind the other.

The men in the second car noted that the first took a direction which would bring them in the direction of Park Lane. They were prepared for a change of plan on the part of the occupant, but he gave no sign. Running along Piccadilly, the man in the second car put out his head.

"Pull up fifty yards this side of the American Embassy," he said, "unless the car goes on."

When it came to the Embassy the first cab turned and slowed down, as though it were going to stop.

It was a clever manoeuvre. The second car halted, obedient to instructions, and the men jumped out, only to see the tail lights of the cab they had been following disappearing at a rapidly increasing rate. In and out of by-streets it turned, traversing the narrow, aristocratic little thoroughfares which abound in that neighbourhood, and it was as much as the pursuers could do to keep it in sight.

They finally lost it in a tangle of traffic in Oxford Street, and the stout man in the second car cursed volubly.

He got out and dismissed the vehicle, and he and his companion, avoiding the well-lighted streets retraced their steps.

"He fooled us all right," said the stout man.

The other grunted. He was a man of few words, this tall, unshaven man, who had a scar on his chin.

"You'd better be getting back," said the stout man vaguely, and, putting his hand in his pocket, gave him some money. "I'm going to see the boss."

Cornelius Helder was strolling idly through Upper Brook Street half and hour later, when the stout man fell in at his side.

"I lost him," he said.

"You're a fool," said the other savagely; "and I suppose you showed your ugly face to every policeman in the City."

"Quit that," said the other. "I have done enough for you lately – too much I think. I have been scared to death this last week seeing my description in the papers."

"You need not worry," said Helder. "There was not one person who described you so that you could be recognized."

"I don't want to be recognized at all," said the other. "It makes me just shiver."

"You've got yourself to blame," said Helder. "All you had to do was to bargain with the old man and get him to sell the stuff at a price."

"I'm nervous," confessed the other. "Say!" – he caught Helder by the arm – "you're the real thing, aren't you? Suppose they got us proper, could you pull us out of it?"

"I guess not," said Helder coolly.

"Then, by God, I'd pull you into it!" said the other fiercely.

"I guess not," said Helder again; "I know nothing. You're mad to worry; you're madder still to threaten me. I've got you like this" – he snapped his fingers as he spoke. "There is not the slightest piece of evidence that would connect me with old Maple's kidnapping. If you squeal, you squeal for trouble."

Under the light of a street lamp he saw the other man's face. It was bathed in perspiration, his mouth was working convulsively.

"I'm not in this," said the man sullenly. "Carl did it because you told him to. He did it for the same reason that I went for old man Gold. You were not in that, I guess – oh no!"

Fortunately, they were passing down a very quiet street. The man's voice was rising in his anger.

"I'm tired of it," he said; "tired of the game. It's God's own country for mine, I'm going back."

"You're not," said Helder quietly.

"I'm going back," said the man doggedly; "I'm through with you."

Helder laughed; there was no need to change his tactics.

"Get religion – you!" he said. "That's not the kind of talk I like to hear from a Chicago 'hold up' man, one of the 'strong arms.' You've nothing to fear, Billy" – he slapped the other on the back – "and you're in sight of glory. Why, in two years you'll be running the handsomest saloon on the east side, with an automobile that will take you out to Coney Island on Sunday afternoons."

But the man was not easily pacified. He was in a strange land, confronted with unfamiliar forces.

It was not until Helder had him snugly ensconced in the corner of a Soho bar that he recovered his equanimity. He even became genial and communicative.

AN EXTRAORDINARY MARRIAGE

There are days in the life of the average man and woman which are so much like other days, so indistinguishable from their fellows, that it is impossible to recall them or to single them out for any happening of moment. Similarly, there are days which mark tragedy or momentous episodes, which stand out, every hour and every moment, in vivid contrast to all others, days that represent a whole period of life. Such a day to all the actors of this story was the fourteenth of May, and it may be set forth almost chronologically.

At seven o'clock in the morning Cornelius Helder walked out of his house in Curzon Street.

It was a bright spring day without a cloud in the sky. He had the appearance of a man who has not slept well; his face had the curious pasty look which comes to a man who spends his nights in close unventilated smoking-rooms. Yet Helder was innocent of any such experience. He was shaven and carefully dressed.

He walked slowly towards the City. The street was given over at that hour to tradesmen, milkmen and scavengers. Very few shops, and these only the less important ones, had taken down their shutters. In Regent Street he saw nothing but hurrying women, little shop girls with parcels under their arms, making their way to their establishments.

He wondered half bitterly what sort of a night Comstock Bell had had. And the girl – where would she be? She would travel up from her suburban home with a third-class ticket, probably in a workmen's train, to be married to one of the richest men in London.

Trivial little thoughts like these passed through his mind. He bought a morning paper, one that usually published quick news. He looked through its columns to see if it contained any news about the arrest of Willetts. There was no mention of the event.

So Comstock Bell was going to wait until he was married and out of the country before he put his treacherous plan into execution. What hold had the girl over him; what was the mystery of this sudden marriage? He had never met her before that day he saw her in his office, and Comstock Bell was not the class of man to lose his head over a pretty face.

There was some solid reason for the marriage; what was it? With an unconscious scowl on his face, he walked swiftly along the sunny side of Regent Street.

At eight o'clock he found himself in the Green Park, the matter of Comstock Bell's marriage still uppermost in his mind. There must be some explanation. Helder was usually a well-informed man; he had no difficulty in discovering where the millionaire was to be married. The ceremony was to be at Marylebone Parish Church and the hour fixed was nine o'clock. Gold, Comstock Bell, and the girl were to meet at the Great Central for breakfast. They were leaving London by the eleven o'clock train for the Continent.

He had no feeling so far as Verity Maple was concerned. He was neither jealous nor chagrined that she, who loathed him, should like Bell sufficiently well to marry him at short notice; he had a theory that if you put the worst construction on people's actions you were in nine cases out of ten right, and he explained her preference by the simple process of comparing his own bank balance with Bell's, not that he ever intended marrying her, or had any thought of matrimony.

He judged that he would meet Gold, because the Green Park on a spring morning was a favourite spot with the detective. He was old enough to have settled habits. Helder expected to find him strolling by the water, and was not disappointed. As Big Ben boomed out the quarter after eight, he saw the American coming toward him.

Gold was never surprised at anything; he was not surprised to see Cornelius Helder. They stopped, speaking together; Gold had a handful of crumbs, which he threw impartially to water-fowl and sparrows.

"I suppose you're to be best man?" said Helder after a time, turning to the other with a smile.

"Something like that," said Gold, his eyes and attention upon the sparrows.

"What is the meaning of it?"

"The meaning of what? Of the marriage?"

"Yes, it's rather an unexpected happening, isn't it?"

"All marriages are unexpected to somebody or other," said Gold.

"Do you think they're a suitable couple?"

"God forbid," said Gold, promptly and piously; "the only two people I ever heard of who carried to the altar the assurance of all their friends that they were made for one another were Adam and Eve, and that was before my time. Affinities only come to married people long after they've been married – to somebody else."

Helder laughed; he was easily amused.

"Spoken like a bachelor," he said, "did you confirm what I told you about Willetts?"

Gold nodded.

"Yes, they will arrest him tonight."

"When Comstock Bell is safely out of the way, eh?" sneered the other. "Say, I'm not proud that he's a compatriot of mine?"

Gold looked at him slyly.

"I haven't heard *him* boasting, for the matter of that," he said; "he's immensely reticent on some subjects."

He looked at his watch.

"I'm going along," he said; "you're not looking well."

"Oh, I'm all right," said Helder; "I'm suffering a little from insomnia."

"You should take up the study of improving literature," said Gold. "Let me advise you to start on a very interesting little book I saw the other day."

"What was it called?"

82

"The Metropolitan Police Code," said Gold; "it is a book of advice intended for young constables and extensively read in criminal circles."

He laughed as if amused with himself; as for Helder, he did not know whether to be amused, alarmed or angry.

The first to reach the hotel were Comstock Bell and the girl. They arrived almost simultaneously. He gave her a smiling welcome. She was grave and, he thought, very beautiful. It is strange that until that moment, when they met in the big Palm Court of the *Great Central Hotel*, he had not thought of her beauty. He had a dim idea that there was something about her which was pleasant to look upon, that her presence was a pleasing experience, but exactly what were the causes which led up to that indefinite and indefinable pleasure he had not known.

Comstock Bell had no love in his heart for any woman, but he was going to marry this girl. It was a marriage of expedience if ever there had been such a marriage in the world. Yet it pleased him, it gave him a sense of comfort, that the woman who was to bear his name, who was to grace his board, and upon whom so much depended, should have been so well favoured by nature. She was dressed in a simple white serge costume, with a little touch of mauve at her waist, and she wore a large shadowy black and white hat.

"We've got about five minutes before the others come," he said, and led her to a seat.

"You don't regret the step you are taking?"

"There is no question of regretting," she said firmly; "when I made up my mind last night, my decision was fixed and irrevocable."

"I – " he began.

"I know," she said, "that you have to tell me something, and that something will be a shock to me. I know that I can help you and that you are marrying me because I can help you, and that I do not love you and that you do not love me. We got into this thing with our eyes open: please God, it will turn out well."

"I can say amen to that," he said solemnly. "Here is Gold."

The detective came down the flight of stairs; it was an unusual sight to see him in a tall hat; it was strange to see him at all so early in the morning. They adjourned to the dining-room. Breakfast was a prosaic meal; the girl had very little appetite, and Comstock Bell ate sparingly. Gold, who had no sense of responsibility, and moreover was not going to get married, ate heartily, for he was a healthy man and had been up since four o'clock that morning, though neither of the people at the table suspected this fact.

"Where do you intend going?" he asked.

"I shall go to Paris from here," said Comstock Bell deliberately, "and then I shall go on to Munich and then to Vienna, possibly to Budapest, and after that my movements are uncertain."

"It is bad luck for you that your finger is no better," said Gold, pointing to the bandaged hand.

Comstock Bell smiled.

"I scarcely notice it," he said, "and I am getting so expert with my typewriter that I shall probably never go back to the old ways of writing letters."

"Are you taking it with you?" asked Gold.

"Yes, I have had one specially made for travelling," he answered, "although I never thought when I gave the order that it would be myself who would use it."

"Madame will probably be able to assist you," said Gold, with a smile at the girl.

"Unfortunately, or fortunately, for her," said Comstock Bell, "she does not understand this keyboard; it is not the universal keyboard."

There was a lull in the conversation, and Bell beckoned to the head waiter. "Bring me a telegraph form," he said.

In a few minutes the man returned with a telegraph form and a writing pad.

"Shall I write it for you?" said Gold.

"No, I think I can manage," said Comstock Bell, flushing slightly. Laboriously he wrote it out. It was addressed to Lauder, Landview Cottage, Gravesend, and the message it carried was one word: "Proceed."

Gold was mildly curious to know what could be the character of a telegram a man might write on his wedding morn, but he did not see it, because immediately he had written it, Comstock Bell folded the form in two and handed it with half a crown to the waiter.

"Let this be sent off at once," he said, "and bring my bill."

In a little time they were out in the street. Bell did not take a taxicab; they walked the short distance which divided them from the church.

Save for a verger and a pew-opener the church was empty, and their footfalls echoed hollowly as they walked down the aisle. As they stood at the altar rails waiting for the clergyman, there came to them the hum of busy London awakening to a day of toil. If Comstock Bell had ever thought about his wedding day he had never imagined anything like this. As to the girl, face to face with the most tremendous happening of her life, she was numbed with the unreality of the situation.

There was another footfall as the minister came down to meet them. He held a little book in his hand and he spoke the solemn words which were to unite them mechanically, almost glibly. The questions were asked and answered; the plain band of gold slipped on her finger, and they adjourned to the vestry to sign the register. The minister said vaguely that it was a fine day and that he hoped we were really at last going to have an English summer. Comstock Bell replied conventionally enough. Gold paid the fee, and tipped the verger, who was one of the witnesses to the marriage, and the couple passed out into the sunlight Mr and Mrs Comstock Bell.

None who saw the party emerge could have guessed that they were witnessing the beginning of one of London's mysteries.

Bell looked at his watch.

"We have got an hour to spare," he said. "All your boxes are at the station, are they not?"

She nodded. He smiled at her kindly.

"I am going to call you Verity; do you mind?"

"I would rather you did," she said.

85

Wentworth Gold was an interested listener. It was very extraordinary, he thought; like the girl, he was impressed by the unreality of the thing.

Here were these two people, bound together for life; the man a millionaire, the girl well outside his social radius. They were talking like people who had only recently been introduced and had little more than the bonds of acquaintanceship to hold them together. He wondered how long the courtship, if courtship there had been, had lasted. He found himself speculating upon her trousseau; how could she have got it together unless there had been at least an understanding between them. Whatever uncertainties existed upon that point, they were dispelled by Bell's next words.

"You can get all your things in Paris," he said.

"I shall not want very much," she replied quietly.

Comstock Bell looked at his watch and laughed, and the girl smiled sympathetically.

"We've got nothing to do for an hour," he said. "Let us go into the park; will you come, Gold?"

Wentworth Gold was not a society man, and knew little about marriage and the giving in marriage. He was not even domestic; he had reached the stage of bachelordom when matrimony was represented to his mind by mysterious conferences between husband and wife as to what they should have for dinner. But he knew that, by all convention, he ought now to make his adieu and leave the happy couple to their own devices.

He had invented a fictitious engagement and was on the point of expressing his regret that he could no longer enjoy the pleasure of their companionship, when Bell made the lie unnecessary, or at least fortuitous.

"We want you to see us off," he said; "if you can be bored for another hour, Verity and I will be very glad."

A taxi carried them to Regent's Park, and they walked by the side of the ornamental waters talking of everything except Bell's immediate plans. As the time grew nearer his departure he fidgeted and was distrait.

A Debt Discharged

Suddenly, without any warning, he turned to Gold.

"I suppose," he asked, "that Helder has told you that I have betrayed this man Willetts?"

Gold was taken aback; he did not know how Bell could have made the discovery.

"He did tell me something of the sort," he admitted. "I do not however, place any great reliance upon what Helder has told me."

"You can in this case," said Bell quietly. "I betrayed Willetts, and I had a good reason for doing so."

"Has he been arrested?" asked Gold.

"Not yet," said the other. "I have arranged that it should not take place till I was out of England."

It seemed a heartless thing to say, an unexpected confession from a man of Bell's principles. Gold admitted to himself a sense of disappointment. There was something unclean in this scheme of the millionaire's; to betray a man, with whatever object, and then to slip out of the country to escape whatever consequences there might be to his treachery.

"I'm glad you told me," he said coldly.

Comstock Bell looked at him, his grave eyes reading the verdict in his face.

"You must think as well of me as you can," he said.

They reached Victoria; a carriage had been reserved for the young couple.

"Au revoir!" said Gold, holding out his hand.

Bell grasped it firmly.

"We shall meet again?"

"I hope so," said Bell. His manner was absent, he was so evidently thinking of something else that Gold was a little irritated. He stole a glance at the bride of the day; it was difficult to tell, such was her wonderful complexion, whether or not she was pale. He thought she was a little; there were dark lines under her eyes which suggested she had not slept well.

He shook hands with her, said the thing that might be expected of the best man taking farewell of a bridal couple, and he stood on the platform till the train was out of sight.

"An extraordinary marriage," he said.

He turned, left the station, and almost ran into Helder, who had also been a spectator.

Gold eyed him disapprovingly.

"If I did not know," he said coldly, "that you were a most honourable and inoffensive man" – he spoke with great deliberation and with offence in every word – "I should say that you had been following us."

The other smiled.

"You would be saying what is true," he said frankly. "I have been watching you. I am as interested in the marriage of Comstock Bell as you are, and I tell you candidly – you can believe me or not as you like it – that I do not know why I am interested."

"You surprise me," said Gold dryly. "Your type of man, I should imagine, never did anything unless he had a very good reason for doing it."

Helder laughed.

"This conduct of mine can be classed as exceptional," he said.

He would have walked with Gold wherever the latter was inclined to go, but the Embassy detective made it clear that he wished to be alone. For that reason he avoided the club, knowing that Helder would be there: for that reason he busied himself with some arrears of work and the preparation of a report for the Treasury at Washington.

He came down to the club to dine, and found two telegrams awaiting him. They were both from Bell: one had been handed in at Dover and was a telegram of thanks for his kindness. The second was from Calais, and the hour of handing in was three o'clock. The message was a curious one. It ran: "Will you see my man Parker tomorrow – I have given him a holiday today – and ask him to forward my letters."

Gold put the telegram down. Why had he not wired direct to Parker? And how came it that such a methodical man as Bell had forgotten to instruct his servants before his departure? He smiled.

"I suppose," he said to himself, "that when young people get married, such little things as readdressing letters escape their attention."

He made a note in his pocket-book to fulfil the commission, and finished his dinner at leisure. He had letters to read which had been forwarded to him from the Embassy, and they were not pleasant letters. He read them philosophically, refolded them, and put them in his pocket.

At another table Helder sat, ostentatiously examining an evening paper. Gold shrewdly surmised that the paper was only a blind. What was Helder's object? He was not the sort of man to waste time in the pursuit of satisfying an idle curiosity. Gold determined to find out. He crossed over.

"I am going for a stroll," he said; "will you come too?"

"With pleasure," said the other, and rose with alacrity.

It had occurred to Gold that he had an engagement the following day, and that he would probably be unable to see Parker. He took an envelope from the writing-room, slipped the telegram into it, and addressed it to the man. It was an excuse for a walk; he would go to Cadogan Square and drop the letter in the box.

The two men left the club together.

"Now, I want to ask you a straight question," said Gold, "and I want a straight answer."

"That sounds formidable," said Helder; "but I will endeavour to oblige you. What is it you wish to know?"

Gold nodded. "Why do the movements of Comstock Bell interest you so keenly?" he asked.

"All people interest me," said Helder.

"But not to the extent of wasting your time, if I know anything about you," said Gold. "There is something more in your interest in Comstock Bell than meets the eye."

They walked a little way in silence; then Helder spoke reluctantly.

"You are a friend of his, and I do not want to annoy you."

"You annoy me more," said Gold, "by hinting at things which you refuse to substantiate."

"Well, I will tell you," said Helder after another pause; "I believe Comstock Bell is what the English call a 'wrong' un.' "

"Is that all?" said the other dryly.

"Is it not enough?"

"The mere fact that you think he is a 'wrong' un' is not enough to convince me that he is what you think he is," said Gold. "I guess if a man were convicted on private opinion of him, the jails of this little country would be filled with miscreants who had offended against what we consider to be good taste. Have you nothing more substantial?"

"I believe he is buying his freedom at the cost of another man's," said Helder solemnly.

Gold smiled. "I think the truth is," he said "that Bell knows something about you that you would rather he didn't, and that you won't be happy in your mind till you see him out of the country."

In the half-darkness Helder's face went red.

"That is an absurd suggestion," he said.

They were in Codogan Square now, and as they approached Comstock Bell's house Gold took the envelope from his pocket.

"I want to slip this into the letter-box," he said. "It is an instruction for Bell's servants."

They came to the house. It was an old-fashioned building, and had been built at a period when a housewife deemed no house satisfactory which did not allow her from her drawing-room window to obtain a very full view of the steps which led from the street to the front door.

"There is somebody waiting on the steps," said Helder suddenly.

Gold looked up.

Standing in the shadow was a young man.

He had evidently just arrived, for he was searching for the electric push.

"Is that Mr Comstock Bell?" he asked.

Gold laughed quietly.

"No" Mr Comstock Bell is out of town."

"Are you a friend of Mr Bell's?" asked the stranger.

"I don't know why –" began Gold.

The young man produced a card.

"My name is Jackson; I am a representative of the *Post Journal*," he said. "We have got information that he was married today."

"A reporter, eh?"

Gold slipped the envelope he had brought into the letter-box before he offered any further comment.

"Yes," he said good-humouredly, "I can tell you as much as I think Mr Bell would like you to know. He was married today, and left for Paris this morning."

"Would you be good enough to tell me the lady's name; it is rather important, isn't it?" he smiled. "You see our public is enormously interested in millionaires and their brides."

Gold hesitated. After all, he thought, there was no reason why the Press should not know – anyway, they could easily find out if he refused the information.

"He was married to Miss Verity Maple," he said.

The reporter whistled.

"Not the niece of the man who –?"

Gold nodded.

"You can forget that part of it, my son," he said.

The journalist placed his notebook in his pocket.

"I have too good a memory to forget Miss Maple," he said dryly. "She was a young lady who, once seen, is not easily forgotten, and I saw her when her uncle made his mysterious disappearance."

They stood on the steps whilst this conversation was in progress. Helder paced to and fro on the pavement, waiting impatiently for the conference to end.

"Thank you very much for your kindness," replied the reporter, turning with Gold to descend the steps, when an exclamation from Helder arrested him.

He was staring past them in the direction of the drawing-room window.

"Look!" he whispered.

Gold followed the direction of his eyes, and was struck dumb with amazement.

For there, standing in the window, a tense, horrified expression on her face, was Verity Comstock Bell, who that morning had been Verity Maple.

She was staring into the street: the light of the street lamp revealed her haggard face; the down-drawn mouth, the eyes staring as though at something they could not see, her brows frowning, such a frown as those who are suddenly confronted with terrible trouble wear.

For a moment she stood thus; then her eyes turned in the direction of the three men, and she stepped back into the darkness.

THE PASSING OF WILLETTS

"Did you see?" gasped Helder. He seemed unnecessarily alarmed by the apparition.

Gold felt his breath come quicker and a cold sweat break upon his body. There was something uncanny in the momentary appearance of a woman who was, by his calculations, three hundred miles away from London, and between whom and himself the sea stretched.

He stood irresolutely at the foot of the steps, made a movement as if to go up, and stopped himself. It was no business of his, though the girl's evident trouble was sufficient excuse.

Then he remembered the reporter.

Jackson had been a silent witness of all that had passed.

Gold saw his eyes blazing with excitement. No hound scenting a fresh trail is comparable with the reporter who finds the thread of a big story. It was out of his hands, now, thought Gold.

He laid his hand on the journalist's arm.

"Mr Jackson," he said, "this is a matter which should go no further. Mr Comstock Bell is a friend of mine, and this sudden appearance of his wife can, I have no doubt, be easily explained."

"I'm sure it can," said the other politely.

He looked at his watch, and Gold's heart sank.

You may bribe most unlikely people, even in incorruptible London; you may "steady" the police – a little; obtain favours in unexpected quarters if you acted discreetly; but nowhere in the English-speaking world, whether it be Nelson, BC, New York,

Johannesburg or London, can you buy the silence of an enthusiastic reporter who has his nose on a big story.

Gold tried a new line.

"Mr Comstock Bell," he said impressively, "is a very rich man, and although the circumstances of tonight are remarkable, they are, as I have said, open to explanation. I can only warn you on his behalf he is sure to take action against any person or newspapers which suggests anything to his discredit."

"I'm sure he would," said the reporter again, more politely than ever, and a trifle verbose; "you may be sure that I shall write what I have to write in that spirit of genial interrogation which is the peculiar characteristic of my paper."

With a curt nod he left them. Gold knew that it was hopeless to attempt to stem any comment in that direction.

He stood watching the reporter till he was out of sight; then he led the way along the square, a silent Helder at his side.

He said nothing; there was nothing to say. He did not speak for ten minutes.

"What does it mean?" asked Helder excitedly. "There is something behind this. I tell you there is foul play somewhere. I know Comstock Bell – he's capable of anything; I'm going to find out."

Gold caught his arm as he turned away.

"Where are you going?" he demanded authoritatively.

"I'm going to the police."

"You may save your trouble," he said curtly. "I have a slight knowledge of journalism, and the police will have all the incentive they want. And, after all," he added dryly, "why should you give the Press a story which would eclipse entirely the reappearance of Mrs Comstock Bell?"

He spoke significantly; there was no mistaking the underlying menace of his words.

"I don't know what you mean," the other said hoarsely.

"You'll find out one of these days, Helder" said the other. "Let Comstock Bell work out his own salvation and do you work out yours."

"What do you mean?" asked the other again.

"Do you work out yours?" repeated Gold, and nodded his head at every word.

Helder lowered his face till it was on a level with the other's, and it was not a pleasant face to look upon.

"Gold," he said, between his teeth, "they tell me you're a detective, a sort of gentlemanly spy, and that your duty is to discover things in places where men of your kidney are not usually admitted. But if you say a word injurious to my reputation, I'll have you hounded out of every club in London. Do you understand that?"

Gold laughed.

"I know you to be a forger," he said calmly, "and I believe you to be associated with the gang which is now flooding the United States with forged five-dollar bills. I tell you frankly that I have no proof against you, and I tell you as frankly that if I had the very hint of a clue to associate you with the crime, I would never rest till I saw you in a States prison. I believe that your Shropshire printing establishment, run in the interests of the down-trodden peasantry of Russia, was a cover for forgeries on a big scale. Now you know exactly how I feel toward you, and you can take what steps you like."

"You have no proof," gasped Helder.

"Proof!" Gold laughed bitterly. "If I had proof, do you think I'd be talking to you except through prison bars? I only want a pennyworth of proof to put you out of mischief."

They stood under the light of a street lamp, and Gold's face was pale. For the first time in his life, he had been trapped into putting a natural enemy upon his guard. He was chagrined, and his nerves were upset. He had received letters from his chief which had annoyed him: the department he had so faithfully and so successfully served had lost its head over this matter of the forged bills.

"I see!" said Helder slowly. "Now that I know your views, I shall take such steps as are necessary to protect myself."

Gold nodded his head.

"You must be the best judge of that," he said. "So far as Mrs Comstock Bell is concerned, I tell you you're at liberty to go to the police, and I warn you that, from your point for view, it would be unwise to call attention to yourself."

He strode off, cursing himself as he walked that he had allowed his irritation and his growing suspicion of Helder to betray him into the *faux pas* he had made.

It would increase the difficulty of his work enormously. He had taken a wrong line throughout. He should have had the Shropshire establishment raided before the *Red Monitor* had ceased publication and the establishment of Russian printers had been dispersed. It was too late now. If it was Helder who put the forged bills into circulation, he was operating from some secret place which so far Gold and his men had been unable to discover.

He went to his flat, still worried. Then he remembered that his own servant knew Parker. He rang the bell, and his man came.

"Cole," he said, "you know Parker, do you not?"

"Parker, sir?" asked the man.

"Yes Mr Comstock Bell's servant."

"Oh, yes! I know him very well, sir."

"Mr Bell has given him a holiday today; where do you think I could find him?"

"At once, sir?" asked the man, surprised.

"Tonight."

"He's probably gone to see his sister," said the man; "she's the only relation he's got in London."

"Where does she live?"

"In Dalston, sir. I've got the address somewhere," said the man.

He went out of the room and came back with the address written on a piece of paper. In the meantime, Gold had formed his plans. He glanced at the sheet.

"Take a taxi to this place, and bring back Parker if he is there. If he is not there, and you can find him, bring him here at any hour of the night."

"I may as well settle this matter at once" said Gold to himself when the man had gone. "Tomorrow the papers would be full of the story."

He tried to read, but the terrified face of the girl he had seen at the window came between him and his book. He put it down, and paced the room restlessly.

The click of the key in the lock told him Cole had returned. He went into the hall. Paker was there in the glory of his holiday raiment.

"Have you got a key of Mr Bell's house?" asked Gold.

"Yes, sir," replied Parker.

"I want you to come with me to the house."

"Is anything wrong, sir?" asked Parker in alarm.

"Nothing, nothing," said Gold impatiently. He did not think it wise to take the man into his confidence.

They drove to Cadogan Square. It was long past midnight, and the streets were deserted. Parker opened the door.

"One moment, sir," he said, and switched on the electric light.

"Go upstairs first. Knock at your master's door and see if he's there."

"But, sir – "

"Go!" said Gold peremptorily.

Parker ran up the stairs. In a few minutes he came back.

"Did you go into the room?" asked Gold.

"Yes, sir."

"Was anybody there?"

"Not so far as I could see, sir," replied Cole.

"What room is that?" asked Gold, indicating a door.

"That's the drawing-room, sir."

"Just open it," he said.

It was unlocked.

"That's very strange," said Parker.

"What's very strange?" asked Gold quickly.

"This door was locked when I left the house."

"Has anyone else a key?"

"Mr Comstock Bell," said Parker. "All the doors have Yale locks fitted into the wood, so that you can hardly see where the lock is, can you?"

Gold examined the door. It was rosewood and, as the man said, it was difficult to see where the key fitted. He took an electric lamp from his pocket and flashed it on the jamb. The keyhole was the tiniest slit in the polished surface of the wood. Gold examined it carefully. There were a number of little scratches, which he judged had been recently made.

"Whoever used the key last was not well acquainted with this door," he said. "You were going to say that Mr Comstock Bell had a duplicate set?"

"Yes, sir," said the man.

Gold opened the door and walked in. The electric switch was on his right. He pressed the knob, and the room was flooded with light. It was empty.

The detective's nostrils widened. "Do you smell anything, Parker?" he asked.

"Yes, sir," said Parker; "there is a sort of scent in the room."

There was a faint odour of violets.

Very carefully he made a search of the room. The furniture was in its place, shrouded with linen. There were burglar alarms on the windows; they had not been interfered with. In the window he saw a flat case. It was about four inches square. He stooped and picked it up and put it in his pocket. He had seen at a glance what it was. It was the case in which Cooks' place the railway tickets they issue, and he knew that Comstock Bell had booked his passage through to Vienna with that agency.

The search of the remainder of the house revealed nothing more. It was empty; nobody was there. Mrs Comstock Bell had disappeared.

"I think that will do, Parker," he said when he had finished his examination.

"Nothing has been touched, sir?" said the man, who had the possibility of burglary in his mind.

"No," said Gold, "nothing has been touched."

He left Parker and drove back to his flat. He thought perhaps the girl had come to him in this absence, but nobody had called.

A cablegram was awaiting him and an express letter.

He opened the latter eagerly, hoping that it was from the girl. It was from Scotland Yard – from Chief-Inspector Grayson.

"We arrested Willetts at eleven o'clock tonight," said the message.

Gold nodded: he had asked Scotland Yard to keep him informed regarding the mysterious Willetts.

The cablegram was more serious. It was from the chief of his department at Washington, and ran:

"Come at once Washington. Consultation. Leave by *Turanic.*"

Gold swore softly. The *Turanic* was due out of the Mersey the following day, and he spent that night in packing, and left London at six o'clock in the morning.

Helder heard of the arrest at the club. The news came by telephone from one of his agents. He was sitting in the reading-room thinking of the events of the night when a telegram was brought to him which had been handed in at New York two hours previously. It was simple:

"Urgent, come to New York by *Turanic.*"

It was signed by the name of the a man whose word was law to Helder, and he went home to make preparations.

Thus it came about that Gold met the last man in the world he desired or expected to meet on the platform at Euston station the following morning. Thus it happened that these two men crossed the Atlantic together, not exchanging a sentence on the voyage.

And whilst Gold and Helder were attending to their business in New York, all London was asking: "Where were the Comstock Bells?"

The *Post Journal* asked it in big type, asked it again in smaller type, double leaded; called it "a remarkable occurrence," "a strange visitation," even went so far as to describe it as "a mystery." Being a wise journal, this paper steered clear of suggesting that there had been any foul play. It speculated upon the possibility of the Comstock Bells having come back to London to spend their honeymoon, and had a little article on London as a honeymoon resort. It hinted at the supernatural, and hoped that nothing had happened to the young people. Then it grew bolder, for its busy correspondents throughout the Continent had been seeking the young people, and had sought unsuccessfully.

Where was Mr Comstock Bell?

His friends treated the matter as a joke, and rival newspapers suggested that the reporter had been mistaken and was desirous of creating a little sensation in an admittedly dull season. Whereupon Jackson sought the two men who had been his companions on the night, only to find they had disappeared from London.

On the sixth day following the publication of his story a letter came to the office of the *Post Journal*. It was dated Lucerne, typewritten on *Swizerhof Hotel* notepaper, and ran:

"Dear Sir, - We have read with a great deal of interest, a little annoyance, and some amusement the speculations of your representative as to where we are spending our holiday, though we were not aware that our movements created so much interest.

"We should be very grateful to you if you would allow us to enjoy the privacy which is our right as individuals. We trust that you will have the courtesy to make this known to the many friends we possess in London, and that your interest in our welfare will now be confined to the silent interest which we feel sure you have in all your readers."

It was signed "Comstock Bell," and underneath, in a feminine hand, "Verity Bell."

The editor of the *Post Journal* handed the letter to the crestfallen Jackson. A big, broad-shouldered man, this editor; grey-haired, clean-shaven, with a voice like the booming of the sea. He growled out a few pleasant curses at his subordinate's head.

"Seems to have made us look pretty foolish, Jackson," he said.

Jackson wisely said nothing. The editor rang a bell, and the chief sub-editor entered. The chief handed him the letter.

"Dress this up," he said. "Explain that whilst we were certain that Mr Bell was well, and there was not much mystery about his disappearance, we were interested in the psychic side of it – "

"But," interrupted Jackson, "would it not be as well to ask our man at Lucerne to confirm that fact that these people are staying there?"

The editor scowled at him.

"I don't know why we should waste any more money and energy on the matter," he said deliberately. "If they find out we are making enquiries they might be unpleasant. It's now eight, and by Swiss time it will be nine o'clock: I doubt whether we should get a reply in time."

"Still, we can try."

At eleven-thirty the chief sub-editor strolled into his superior's room.

"It's a pity the Comstock Bell mystery has fallen through," he said, taking a chair facing the other's desk. "There's very little news of any kind worth printing tonight."

"So I observe," said the other dryly. "Was there nothing at the Old Bailey?"

"One or two cases," said the other carelessly. "A man named Willetts has been charged with the forgery of a £50 banknote."

That's an unusual case; can't you make anything of that?" said the editor.

The chief sub-editor shook his head.

"Happened somewhere about ten years ago," he said, "and the man pleaded guilty. There was nothing sensational about the circumstances. It was forged in Paris, and seems to have been the only one of its kind."

"What did he get?"

"A year's hard labour," said the chief sub-editor.

"Let me see!" The editor rubbed his chin reflectively. "Was not that the time when a number of young men started a crime club?"

The sub-editor nodded.

"It did not come out in the evidence, so we can't give it," he said. "I think the best thing to do is to make Parliament the big story of the day."

A boy brought a telegram and handed it to the sub-editor. He looked at it and read it carefully; then he passed it on to his chief.

"H'm" said the editor, "that's curious."

The telegram read:

"Neither Mr nor Mrs Comstock Bell has been seen at Lucerne, and neither is nor has been staying at the *Swizerhof.*"

They sat without speaking for a minute.

"Who is this from?" asked the editor.

"It is from one of our own men who is taking his holiday at Lucerne. I thought it would be best in a case like this not to depend upon the local correspondent."

The editor touched his bell.

"This is good enough," he said. "Tell Mr Jackson I want to see him," as the messenger came in answer to the bell. "Jackson can work this story up; we have ample material."

At that moment Jackson entered, and the editor passed the telegram to him.

"Get a column out of this, and do it quick," he ordered.

AN ARREST

Wentworth Gold returned to England at the end of May. His visit to Washington had been more satisfactory than he had hoped. The officials recognized the difficulty of his task, and were almost sympathetic. He learnt that he had been suddenly sent for as the result of an unexpected communication from the White House, which gave no reason why he should be summoned and contented himself with the uncompromising instruction that he was to be brought to America immediately.

He had not seen Helder during his stay in Washington, but he knew that he was the kind of man who spent the greater part of his life crossing and recrossing the Atlantic between Liverpool and New York. Such men frequently never go outside the city's confines.

He did not know that Helder's visit had been a critical one; that the big criminal organization was alarmed to the point of panic, and that Helder had travelled out at such short notice because the heads of the organization had received definite information that unless its plan of campaign was considerably modified, it stood in grave risk of detection.

Helder preceded Gold by a few days.

Returning to England, Gold had time to consider the mystery of Comstock Bell. The American newspapers had made more of the disappearance than the London press, and Gold had had little chance of forgetting that he was a friend of Comstock Bell's.

The main clue that Gold had to work upon was the discovery he had made in the house in Cadogan Square. This was the little folder in which Cook's issue their tickets. The two vouchers were there intact, with the exception that the counterfoils which carried the passengers from London to Dover and from Dover to Calais had been extracted. For the rest of the journey so far as Vienna, the tickets remained. But for the fact that the railway coupon and the boat ticket had been detached, there was the possibility that Bell had left them behind. But the ticket from Calais to Amiens had been punched, accidentally possibly, by the inspector at Victoria. That disposed of the suggestion that they had been left behind in the hurry of departure.

Gold quite expected to hear on his arrival in London that Comstock Bell had returned. He was astounded to find half a dozen letters from the man himself awaiting him. One was addressed from Paris the day following the arrival of the married pair. Another letter, with the post date of Lucerne, typewritten on *Swizerhof* notepaper, told of their passage, gave sketchy details of the journey, described the weather, and hoped, conventionally enough, that London was better favoured. The third letter was from Vienna – the thing was a mystery. None of the letters spoke of the lost tickets – a little item which usually annoys a traveller, however rich he may be. Gold candidly admitted to himself that he could not understand it.

Your professional detective, if he is worth his salt, has no friends in business hours. And Wentworth Gold was a professional detective, none the less so because his social position was assured, or because he dealt with irregular happenings in high places. His instinct of the law was greater than any other he possessed. If Comstock Bell had been his own brother, he would have set himself as readily and as unhesitatingly to work to discover the wherefore of his curious behaviour.

A note from Scotland Yard brought him to the Assistant-Commissioner's office.

Captain Symons was a man of considerable ability; he had won his position as chief of the Criminal Investigation Department by sheer merit. A spare, lean man, slightly bald, with a pair of steady blue eyes that looked you through and through, and a light moustache; he was one of the most famous men in London.

He rose as Gold entered his private office and pushed forward a chair.

"Sit down Gold," he said. "I have sent for you to ask you to help me in this Comstock Bell affair. The papers are making a great deal of it; they would make more if they knew as much as we do."

Gold looked out of the window on to the Embankment.

"I don't exactly see," he said with some show of resentment, "why they should bother or even why they should be interested."

The Commissioner smiled grimly.

"Do none of the circumstances appear strange to you?" he said.

"They are a little strange, but how do you mean?"

"I mean, don't you connect Bell's disappearance with the other matters which interest you very much just now?"

"You mean the forgeries?" said Gold in some surprise. "No; why?"

"I don't as a rule," said the Commissioner thoughtfully, "take much notice of anonymous letters; but the letters I have received recently on this matter are so detailed, and contain so much matter which I know to be true, that I cannot afford to ignore them. And there are suggestions in these letters which deserve consideration."

"Such as –" asked Gold.

"Does it not seem strange," repeated the Commissioner, speaking very emphatically, "that the two people who could have furnished the means for detecting these forgeries have both disappeared. One was the man Maple –"

"And the other?" asked Gold.

"The other," said the Commissioner, "is of course, his niece."

"But she –"

"She probably knew the constituents of Maple's mysterious preparation. It is hardly likely that she would live in the same house, sharing his confidence, without knowing exactly how that mixture was made. Within seven days of Maple's disappearance, Comstock Bell, unexpectedly and for no reason that I can imagine, married the girl – a girl considerably beneath him in social status."

Gold was concerned: such a suspicion had come to him, only to be dismissed from a sense of loyalty to his absent friend.

"It is strange," he admitted; "yet it is possible that some simple explanation can cover it."

"I wish I knew what it was," said the Commissioner. "Anyway, we have got to find out. The newspapers are demanding that we should discover that whereabouts of Comstock Bell, and more particularly of Mrs Comstock Bell, who left London on her wedding day, is seen in town the very night when she should be in Paris, and was in Paris, according to Bell's statement to the Press – for she *was* in London, was she not?"

He looked sharply at Gold.

Gold nodded.

"Yes, she was in London," he said seriously.

The situation had developed beyond all considerations of friendship.

"We have set ourselves two tasks," said the chief of the police. "One is to discover the whereabouts of Verity Maple that was – Verity Bell she is now – and the other is to find her disreputable uncle. And my view is that, when these two disappearances are accounted for, we shall have gone a long way to account for the mystery of the wholesale forgeries which are driving your business people to the verge of panic. I thought I would like to let you know exactly what we are doing; I feel I may count upon your co-operation."

Gold inclined his head.

"I also shall work to that end," he said. "I shall want two more men."

"You can have as many as you like," said the Commissioner. "Will you have them now, or shall I give them their instructions?"

"No, they can see me tonight. I wish them to keep a man named Helder under observation."

"Helder?" The Commissioner's eyebrows rose a little.

"Yes," said Gold quietly, "the writer of the anonymous letters."

They looked at one another for a space, then a slow smile dawned on the Commissioner's face.

"When I said anonymous," he said carefully, "I meant they were anonymous to everybody except myself. My acquaintance with you,

Mr Gold, has considerably increased my respect for the American police."

"It was Helder, of course?" said Gold.

The other man led the way to the door and opened it.

"I forget," he said vaguely. "I never remember names."

Gold passed out into the busy street. He had made his plans, and he determined to lose no time in putting them into execution.

English police methods were good, but they were not his methods. He could trust them to watch Helder; but, for himself, he was prepared to act illegally to punish the lawless. If Comstock Bell were indeed head of this organisation – he set his teeth.

He had known such cases; men who were rich beyond the necessity for exertion, who, obeying some perverse instinct, had followed a lawless career, at first for the fun of it, and the excitement of it, and the thrill of it, and then, when they had woven about themselves so close a mesh that they could not escape from its entanglements, in the desperate hope of transferring the burden of their folly to other shoulders.

He kept the telegraph wires busy all that afternoon; his agents, operating in divers parts of the European Continent, answered one by one.

At nine o'clock that night he set out from the flat, accompanied by two men. The night was cold, and a chill east wind made an overcoat necessary for the most robust. The three found a motor car waiting for them in a side street off the Strand. Without any instructions to the chauffeur they took their seats.

"Have you got the warrant?" asked Gold, addressing the two men.

The taller of the two nodded.

"It is the Russian?" asked Gold suddenly.

"Yes, sir," said one of the men. "There was no mistaking him – he had a scar on his chin. He had been drinking, I think. I followed him from Soho to the Great Central Station. There he met the American."

"And from there you followed them to their homes?"

"No," replied the other briefly; "we lost the American."

The car ran eastward through the City; it passed through the crowded High Street of Whitechapel, along Commercial Road, past famous Sidney Street, and pulled up at the corner of a narrow thoroughfare.

"I have chosen this place," explained Gold; "there is the stage door of a music hall down here, and the appearance of a motor car will not excite any extraordinary attention."

One of the men led the way. They passed the stage door, turned into another street, crossed the road and found themselves in one of those populous little thoroughfares which abound in the East End of London.

The neighbourhood was of the poorest and most squalid. In spite of the lateness of the hour, hordes of children thronged the pavements and sidewalks. Half the doors were open, revealing black cavities unlit by the common tenants. In some, women were standing in little groups, discussing the great-little events which made up their sordid lives.

The appearance of three men in a street where the visits of the police are not infrequent, created little more than idle speculation.

Walking sharply, the detectives led Gold to a street which was poorer and even more dilapidated than the first. There were fewer people here; one or two of the doors were closed; before one a man stood.

"This is it," said the man.

Gold stepped forward and pushed the door gently. It opened to his touch. In these small houses, occupied by two, three, and sometimes four families, it is inexpedient to lock the front door.

Gold entered: the other men followed. He had not taken a step when the door leading from the passage into what he judged was the front room, opened, and a man came out.

"Hullo!" he said suspiciously.

Gold flashed the light on him from the little electric torch he carried in his hand.

"Where's the Russian?" he asked.

Gold knew that amongst people such as these names were of no consequence, and that people were best known by their nationality or physical peculiarities.

"Upstairs," said the man, evidently relieved the find that he was not the object of their visit.

"Back or front?" asked Gold.

"Back, sir," said the man. "It's the first room you come to when you reach the landing."

Gold ascended the stairs two steps at a time, the men following.

He reached the door and tried it gently. It was locked. He rapped softly on the panel. At first there was no answer. He rapped again. They heard the rumbling and the creaking of a bed, and the sound of feet on the bare floor. He rapped a third time.

"Who's there?" growled a surly voice.

Gold whispered something loudly in a language which the two men did not understand.

He waited: the door was unlocked and opened a little.

Gold thrust the door back and entered. It was his man; he recognized him from the description. He had been drinking, and was sleeping off the effects of the drink when the knock came.

"Who are you?" he asked.

"Light a lamp, somebody," ordered the detective.

One of the men struck a match and found a tin petroleum lamp, removed its shade, and lighted it.

The room was a miserable compartment, containing a dingy bed and little else.

"I want you," said Gold, speaking in Russian. "Take your hand from you pocket." He spoke quietly, but the revolver he thrust to the Russian's diaphragm supplied all the violence that the occasion called for. "Put up your hands!"

Sullenly the man raised his hands above his head, and Gold and his attendants scientifically disarmed him. A pair of handcuffs were snapped on his wrists behind him.

"Sit down on that chair," said Gold. "We shall do you no harm and by and by you must tell us all you know."

"I will tell you nothing," said the man.

Quickly they made a search of the room and of the contents of the man's pockets. There was nothing to indicate his association with any person, and neither letters nor papers of any description. One of the men had disappeared whilst the search was in progress, and when Gold had blown out the lamp and had guided the prisoner downstairs, they found the motor car waiting for them.

The Russian was bundled in; the car was running westward again before the people of Little John Street awoke to the realization that there had been an arrest made in their midst.

MRS BELL LISTENS

The room was a large one. It had been used as a cabinet-maker's workshop before the influx of an alien population, and the inevitable rise in rent values had driven the artisan further east to Poplar and Canning Town, and had made such a business address an expensive luxury to the struggling tradesman who had rented it.

At little benches men sat working silently, carefully. In a corner of the room, separated by a screen of match-boarding, a little machine went "click-click-click" monotonously, insistently.

Most of the workmen were foreigners, and they were engaged in perfectly legitimate business, the engraving of plates for fine art reproductions, a delicate process, requiring a steady eye and a sure hand. Such records as we now possess tell us that the plates and the pictures that were pulled from them found a ready sale on the Continent – the subjects were not suitable for the English purchaser.

Nor had the little oblong slips which the concealed machine was throwing out evenly and regularly much currency in England, for they were five-dollar notes, perfectly printed.

The machine was a small one, smaller than the usual banknote printing machine. It had a multitude of rollers and dampers and ink ducts confined within its limited proportions, and with the bills which it printed no fault could be found.

A thick-set man sat on a high stool by the side of the machine, the butt of a cigar in the corner or his mouth, his soft felt hat on the back of his head, and his hands thrust deep into his trouser pockets.

He watched the machine earnestly, following every movement of the white-smocked workmen who collected the notes in little bundles and deftly bound them together. When a hundred such bundles had been printed he stretched out his hand, switched off the current and the machine stopped.

"That will be enough for tonight," he said.

He pushed the notes to one side and stood waiting whilst the plates from which they were printed where removed, carefully cleaned and wrapped in tissue paper. A man handed him the plates and he slipped them into his inside pocket. He watched till the workmen had replaced them with four steel cuts which made up a Lager beer label, tucked the remainder of the banknote paper under one arm and the finished notes under the other, and opened a little door which led to what had been in other days the master carpenter's office.

He unlocked a safe that stood in the corner and put the bundles carefully inside, locking the great steel door afterwards.

From a cupboard he took a bottle and a glass. He had reached the stage when wholesale forgery was getting on the wrong side of his nerves. There had been too many alarms, too many breathless hours of fear. He took a long drink and replaced the bottle.

The workshop stood over some stables; beyond a door facing that which led from the workshop into the room was an outside staircase. He switched off the light, unlocked the door and looked out; then he closed it again, turning the key.

Tomorrow those notes, neatly packed in two-hundred separate envelopes, addressed by two hundred separate agents, would be sent by post to the United States. Every day that week the same post would be dispatched.

It was a larger consignment he had on hand than usual. The plates would last for another long printing, after that the new plates, which an unwilling worker was preparing, would be employed.

He looked at his watch. It was a quarter to nine. He went through the little printing office to the larger room.

"You can finish for tonight," he said.

The hours of his establishment were irregular. It was in accordance with his plans that, when the tiny machine was about its nefarious work, the members of his staff should be effectively engaged on the premises.

Only two men were in the secret of the business besides himself and his immediate boss. The printer was one: he was employed elsewhere during the day and was a safe man. Helder had chosen him with care.

As to the second man – Tiger Brown shook his head with a little frown, for the second man and the thought of him kept him awake at nights and drove him to the little bottle in the cabinet.

There was a soft tap on the door. Again he turned out the light and opened it carefully.

"It's all right." Helder stepped in and closed the door behind him.

"Have you been working?"

"I've just finished," said the other.

"Get the stuff away tonight if you can," said Helder. He was in a palpably nervous state.

"What's wrong?" asked the other sharply.

"I don't know what's wrong," he said testily, "only I've a feeling that I'm being watched."

"Why do you come here, then?" growled the other.

"I had to see you tonight," said Helder, speaking rapidly. "Brown, this thing is getting too much for us. I want you to print every bit of paper you've got and destroy the plate. I'm going to close down this establishment."

The other nodded.

"We've had a long run," he said; "I'm worried myself. Ivan has been arrested."

"Arrested?" Helder turned with a start. "Who arrested him? When?"

His face was deathly white, his hands clenched and unclenched in his agitation.

"If he talks," he said, "we're finished; and if I know anything of that man Gold he'll make him talk. Where is he?"

"Ivan? I don't know. I haven't been the round of the police stations; it is not exactly a hobby of mine, calling on the police. We shall know tomorrow all right."

"Why did you not send me word?" asked Helder, and swore softly. "Providing Ivan will keep silent we can win out. The police half believe that Comstock Bell is in this. They are searching Europe for him, and whilst they are looking for him they won't be troubling us."

"Suppose he turns up?" asked Brown.

"I have an idea he won't turn up," replied the other with a little smile. "I've a suspicion, and tomorrow I'm going to make perfectly sure. Already all London – that part of London which is worthwhile – believes Comstock Bell to be concerned in the forgeries."

"What does London know about the forgeries?" asked Brown. The other looked at him in surprise.

"You don't read the papers, my friend," he said, "otherwise you'd know. The American Government has offered – "

He stopped. Was it wise to tell this man that a reward of a million dollars had been offered for the arrest and conviction of the leaders in this speculation.

"Offered what?" asked Brown again.

"They have offered a big reward," said Helder steadily. After all the man would find out by purchasing a paper. "To any person other than those actually engaged in the forgeries." He emphasized the last sentence. "That cuts out you and I."

Tiger Brown went to the cupboard, produced his bottle and almost automatically filled a glass. Helder watched him, interested. Brown was a problem; he was a danger too, and Helder had no intention of resigning his liberty and the loss of all he had gained with such labour and cunning for this boorish confederate of his.

"What are you going to do with Maple?" asked Brown.

"That's what I've come to see you about," said the other.

He strode up and down the little apartment, his hands behind his back.

"We'll go and see him tonight – " He stopped and listened.

"What was that?" he asked.

"I heard nothing," said the other irritably; "the men are leaving and they make a little noise."

Helder crept up to the door leading to the outside staircase and listened.

"There's somebody outside," he whispered.

"You're mad," said the other; "there's nobody there."

He switched out the light, turned the key and flung the door open quickly.

The landing was deserted. Helder stepped out and peered into the dark yard below.

"There's somebody down there," he said.

He saw a figure glide in the dark shadow of the wall; it made for a little doorway which led out to a back street at the rear of the premises. Brown whipped out a revolver, but the other caught his hand.

"You fool," he said, "do you want the whole of London at your heels? After him."

He went down the steps quickly: as he reached the ground he heard the click of a lock and saw the door opened by the small cloaked figure. He stopped and shouted. He ran across the intervening space, only to have the door slammed in his face.

"Have you got a key?"

Brown fumbled in his pocket, produced the key, inserted it in the lock with a shaking hand, and opened the door.

The two men gained the street and looked up and down. Helder caught a glimpse of the fleeing figure of the eavesdropper as he passed under the lamp.

"It's a boy," he said; "we've got to get him. Run!"

The figure disappeared round a corner, and the two men sprinted after it. They turned the corner, they were in another long street. Half-way down, drawn up beside the pavement, was a motor car. Their quarry leapt into it, and the car moved on.

"Quick!" said Helder, "my own car is at the end of this street."

He ran at top speed, found his car waiting, had breath to gasp a few directions, for he was not an athletic man and was unused to violent exercise, and then jumped in, followed by Brown.

He took some time to recover his breath.

"It's lucky," he said, "my car was waiting; we'll be able to track our young friend."

"Do you think he heard anything?"

"I'm certain he did," said Helder; "he was on the landing outside the door."

"What could he have heard?" asked Brown.

"The fact that he was listening is sufficient for me," said Helder grimly.

He let down the front window which separated them from the chauffeur.

"Are you keeping the car in sight?" he said.

"Yes, sir," said the man; "it was held up by a block of traffic near Aldgate."

The car passed through the City, down Queen Victoria Street, along the Embankment.

Helder's heart beat faster as they approached the Westminster end of the great boulevard. On the right was a big block of buildings, famous the world over.

"If he goes into Scotland Yard," he said, "we've got to skip, and quickly."

The car did not drive into the arched entrance of the police head-quarters. It turned sharply to the left, over Westminster Bridge. On the Surrey side it stopped; the pursuers came up as its occupant stepped out quickly and reached the broad flight of stairs which led down to the river.

"We've got him," said Helder.

He ran down the steps after the little figure, reached the broad, wide landing, and halted. For at the bottom of the steps, clear to be seen in the bright light of a bridge lamp, was Verity Comstock Bell, behind her a skiff with two men seated in it.

"I think you had better go back, Mr. Helder," she said.

116

She held an automatic pistol carelessly in both hands, as a woman holds a closed fan.

"And I think," she added, "it would be wise of you if you made every effort to undo the mischief you have caused by associating my husband with your wicked work."

THE MESSAGE OF THE BILL

On the 14th of July, 192–, the cashier employed in Cook's Paris Office in the Place de l'Opéra received five French notes of a thousand francs, and eight American notes for a hundred dollars with the request that they might be changed into English currency.

He counted them carefully, made certain calculations on a piece of scribbling paper, and drew from a wallet beneath the counter the requisite number of English banknotes to make the exchange. It was necessary to add two pounds, a few shillings and two or three pence to make up the amount.

He placed the English money on the counter before him and again counted the French and American paper, and then saw, for the first time, that the words "Banque Nationale" were not the precise shade of violet to which his skilled eyes were accustomed. This was only on one of the notes. He compared the minus-violet note with its fellows, and was more than ever convinced that something was wrong.

Before he moved any further in the matter he examined the American notes carefully. They did not differ in any respect from one another, but to make absolutely sure he took a hundred-dollar bill from his deposit and compared it, and again found there was just the slightest shade of difference.

Now the peculiarity of banknotes printed in France is that they do not retain the exact shade in which they are printed. A week after printing, and before they are issued, they mellow to an indefinable extent.

The cashier at Cook's pushed a little bell beneath the counter and the middle-aged gentleman who was waiting impatiently for his change, suddenly found himself with a detective on either side.

"Would monsieur be good enough to step into the manager's office?"

Monsieur had no desire to step into the manager's office. He spoke very loudly with a distinct American accent, and turned to walk from the offices. This was a false move on his part, because no sane man, however annoyed he might be with money-changers, would ever think of abandoning in his pique four banknotes for a thousand francs each, and five American hundred-dollar bills.

The persuasive touch on either arm became a firm grip. To the scandal of the other clients of that distinguished firm he was hustled into a side room and the door was locked. A quarter of an hour later he left by a side entrance in the custody of two detectives.

Gold, who at that moment was engaged in securing the documents necessary for the search of Helder's flat, left by the first available train for Paris.

A chief of the detective department met him at the Gare du Nord, and they drove together to the Prefecture; on the way, the officer explained many points which it had been deemed inexpedient to embody in the telegram which summoned the American to Paris.

"We are not quite certain about the American notes," he said; "there is no doubt whatever that the French notes are very clever forgeries. The man we have is an American; he arrived at Havre last Saturday with letters of introduction to various American Ministers in Europe. If it were not for his anxiety to escape, we should regard him as the innocent victim of some clever forgers."

"What is his name?" asked Gold.

"Schriener," said the other. "He says he is a New York hardware merchant on a holiday in Paris. The New York police have traced him; he keeps travelling in a much better state than a man of his circumstances could afford. We have searched his baggage."

"And have you found anything?" asked Gold.

"Nothing particularly suspicious," said the other, with some hesitation, "though there are one or two points which require a little explanation. We should like you to see him first. I might say that he has already communicated with the American Ambassador in Paris."

Gold nodded; he knew that the American abroad, whether he be millionaire or crook, lost little time if he were in trouble before he began to disturb the rest of his country's representative.

The man had not been placed in a cell. Gold found him in a little office of the Prefecture which had been turned into a temporary lodgement. He was sitting writing furiously when Gold entered. The detective saw a man of middle height, grey-haired and well-dressed. He was probably about fifty years of age, hard featured, and by no means prepossessing.

"How do you do?" said Gold, and offered his hand.

The hand Gold grasped was a rough one; it was not the hand of wealth or of one who had spent much of his life in ease. Moreover, there was a certain hesitation in the response which told the American that the prisoner was not over-used to social intercourse, and the brief conversation which Gold had with him confirmed this view. The man was a puppet. He was a tough, too. Gold judged this much from his wealth of language. He was exhaustively voluble, too voluble for his safety.

Gold left him to go to the chief detective's office to inspect the notes. The little dossier was handed to him and he examined the bills carefully. When he had finished he returned them.

"There is no doubt at all," he said; "these are very clever forgeries. Will you let me see the man's belongings?"

They were in the adjoining room, labelled and ticketed.

"All the documents," said the French detective, "are together. Would you like to see them?"

Gold nodded, and a number of papers were spread on the table before him.

They were, for the most part, of an ordinary character: notes of credit for small amounts, letters of introduction to consuls and ministers signed by fairly well-known men in New York. To these

Gold attached little importance, knowing the ease with which such letters could be obtained.

There was a notebook with a number of entries. These mainly related to hotels and pensions. More important was a list of firms which Gold knew were places where money could be changed.

The most important clue was an envelope addressed to the man at the Palace Hotel. It bore the London postmark, and was a very ordinary envelope, oblong in shape, and the address was written in a clear hand.

Gold turned to the Frenchman.

"You are watching the hotel premises?" he said.

The other nodded.

"I don't think there will be much of a result," Gold said. "The *modus operandi* is invariably the same. The forged notes are sent in small quantities in such an envelope as this to an agent. A reasonable time is given him to dispose of the forgeries. He remits a portion of the profits to headquarters, which is not necessarily the same place from whence the forged bills come, and then, as I say, after a reasonable interval, another small batch is sent to him."

"And you think," asked the Frenchman, "that we may expect a further supply of notes to arrive at the hotel?"

"No, I don't," he said. "In the first place, every agent of the gang is watched by another agent unknown to him. The second agent is as well paid as the first. By this time the forger knows that Schriener has been arrested. You need not expect any further consignment."

Gold took up the envelope containing the forged American bills, and again subjected one of them to a close scrutiny.

"Beautifully done," he said. He looked at it back and front. Something attracted his attention, and he peered earnestly at one corner of the bill.

"Excuse me," he said quickly, taking the note to the window.

Paris lay under grey skies, and the light was bad. But he saw running from one side of the bill to another a curious line. It was printed in the same mauve ink which formed the background of the note, and was to all appearances part of the design.

"I want a strong light and a reading glass," he said, sharply.

The chief of the detective force switched on a powerful electric light over his desk and pulled down the shade till it nearly reached the table below.

From his drawer he produced a powerful magnifying glass and handed it to Gold. The American detective spread the note on the desk, and, holding it in its place, examined it.

They heard a whistle, saw the colour mount to his cheeks, and his eyes blazed with excitement.

"Look!" he said.

The Frenchman took the glass from him and uttered an exclamation, for the line was writing of minute smallness engraven with extraordinary cunning, and it ran:

"Verity Maple, 942 Crystal Palace Road, London, note numbers 687642 to 687653 milk."

They looked at each other, the two men.

"What does it mean?" asked the Frenchman, bewildered.

Gold was staring out of the window. He made no reply. He was repeating the message of the bill.

"There is one person in the world who can elucidate that message," he said: "she must be found."

"But who wrote it?" asked the chief of the police.

"Who else but Tom Maple?" Gold answered. "I think we are going to discover things."

THE HOUSE PARTY AT
COLLETT'S FOLLY

Between Cambridge and Waltham Cross there are three crossroads. One is the main road into Cambridge; the other carries the traveller to Newmarket and beyond; the third is of little account, being but a wandering wagon track which winds and twists southwards. Of so little account is it that those responsible for the traveller's guidance have not deemed it necessary to put up a board informing the curious as to whither this shabby road leads.

Locally it is chiefly remarkable as an evidence of old Collett's Folly – such is the name it bears. Collett had been an eccentric farmer until he died; he carried his eccentricity to the borderline of genius; might have made his name famous throughout agricultural England as a pioneer of scientific farming, but for a kink which kept him short of his goal, if goal indeed he had. This kink manifested itself in expensive forms, and eventually old Collett had died, a ruined man, but supremely happy with the result of his life's experiment. Like many another man who has earned title to fame, his reforms were in the main outrages; whatever other farmers did he regarded *ipso facto* as wrong, and set about to secure a like result by methods which were directly opposite.

It is fact that sixty per cent of old-fashioned methods cannot be improved, twenty-five per cent are susceptible to variation, and the remainder are altogether wrong. Old Collett, applying the principle that the whole hundred per cent demanded a drastic and immediate reform, came to grief.

He left behind him a hundred acres of sick land, a farmhouse which he had built according to his own plans, a mile-long private road, and a weary executor overburdened with posthumous instructions. That unhappy man might have found relief through the Courts of Chancery, but he preferred the illegal and simpler methods of interpreting the dead man's wishes; and disposed of the farmhouse to the first bidder. To his surprise, the offer which came to him was a singularly handsome one. Somebody has prospected the neighbourhood, had discovered in the farmhouse and its grounds something that fulfilled his requirements, and had bought the estate lock, stock and barrel.

Describing the purchaser, Mr Hazlett, the executor, spoke of him as a pleasant American who had taken a fancy to the farmhouse, and was going to turn it into a weekend resort. He did not intend to farm, so he told Mr Hazlett, but he had the house put into a thorough state of repair, repainted and furnished.

It would not be every man's idea of a weekend cottage; it was certainly not that of the executor's. The house was too gloomy, too thick of wall, too suggestive of a prison. From the outside it was a model of ugliness, possessed of all the unattractive features, with geometrical windows at regular intervals, had a door like that of a jail, and, to complete the illusion, all the windows were barred. It was certainly less unattractive inside. The living-room ran from floor to roof; there was a gallery round; for there had been an organ there – the eccentric farmer had been something of a musician. The principle and only bedroom, intended as such, was on the ground floor.

There was a strong-room upstairs, beyond the reach of thieves, with its steel-cased walls. This was approached from the bedroom by means of a ladder, for of stairway there was none. The American purchaser would seem to have been satisfied with this arrangement; certainly he had made no attempt to build in a stairway. The strong-room, with its concrete floor, was reached either from the ground floor bedroom, or through the steel doors opening from the balcony which ran round the tall dining-room. There was a simple stairway here.

The safe, wherein the old man had kept his money – he neither trusted nor patronized banks – was embedded in a thick party wall, and the new tenant found this receptacle very useful. His visits were irregular, so the neighbourhood noted. He employed no hands upon his estate. One old woman, brought some distance, probably from London by her accent, kept the house in order. Even her services were unexpectedly dispensed with after a while, and the new owner of Collett's Folly seemed to manage very well without her. His visits were fleeting; he never spent more than one night at the farm.

Then of a sudden it was noticed that the house was inhabited. A sulky-looking man was seen about the fields; smoke rose daily from the one chimney-pot the house possessed. Almost daily a visitor drove down from London, turned in at the narrow road which led to the Folly, stayed for an hour or two, and then went spinning back towards London. Sometimes it was the owner, sometimes his lieutenant. They never came together until the night when Verity Bell made her dramatic reappearance.

Through the pelting rain Helder drove to his country house – himself at the wheel – Tiger Brown at his side. Neither man spoke during the journey. At two o'clock in the morning Helder slowed down the car as he came to the crossroads, turned into the lane and brought the machine to a standstill before the gloomy exterior of the farmhouse. At the sound of the car the door opened and a man came out. He disappeared and returned with the key of an outhouse; into this Helder guided the car.

Inside the lofty living-room a fire was burning, though it was June, and the two men, wet through and chilled, stood for a moment in silence before the grateful blaze, the third man watching them stolidly.

"Our business will take us some time," said Helder suddenly; have you got a change of clothes for Tiger?"

He turned to the farm's custodian as he asked the question, and the sulky man nodded. Helder went to his own room, pulled open a drawer which contained a complete change, dressed himself rapidly and came to the sitting-room, to find Tiger in the last stages of his toilet.

They talked together in low tones, though the custodian of Collett's Folly said little save to answer laconically the questions which were put to him. He was a small man, with a bushy grey beard and shaggy eyebrows which almost hid the keen eyes that glanced from one to the other with quick, almost bird-like, rapidity.

"What is he doing now?" asked Helder.

The bearded man shrugged his shoulders.

"Foolishness," he said. He was evidently a man who did not waste words.

"What particular form of foolishness?" demanded Helder impatiently.

The third man shook his shoulders again.

"Just drawing and drinking," he said. "Will you see him?"

Helder nodded.

Slipping a key from his pocket the little man led the way. Helder addressed him as Clinker. He mounted a flight of steps which brought the party to the balcony, opened the steel door which led to the strong-room, and stepped in. Helder followed.

The room was lighted by a powerful oil lamp, which swung from the ceiling. It had been roughly furnished with a table and chair and truckle-bed.

By the table sat a man in his shirt and trousers who half turned as the party entered. The table was covered with engraver's tools and a half-finished plate was clamped on the drawing board before him.

"Well, Maple?" greeted Helder.

Tom Maple, straggling beard at this chin, smiled weakly and half rose.

"Are you going to let me out?" he asked in a shaky voice. "I have done what you asked me to do; more than you asked, and I'm sick of this."

Helder patted him on the back.

"I'll let you out all right," he said. "It's your own fault you are here."

The prisoner had been ill; it did not require an experienced eye to discover the fact. His hands, save when he grasped his delicate tools, shook nervously. His weak mouth was all a-twitch. It seemed incredible that those hands, tremulous, unsteady, could have engraved the beautiful work upon the plate.

Helder looked at it and shook his head.

"You can cut that out," he said, "we have done with the French and American bills; all Europe is on the look-out for them. We are going to have one last flutter and finish. Maple, you've got to do us English notes, and they've got to be the crowning effort of your life."

Maple thrust his hands into his pockets, and hunched himself in his chair. There was a new and strange determination in the under-hung jaw, in the lines about his mouth. Helder saw it, and was a little apprehensive.

"Look here, Maple," he said, "you're not going to turn squeamish; I thought you had got over that. For a man who has perpetrated some of the cleverest forgeries the world has ever known, you are a singularly uncertain quantity. You owe us a grudge for bringing you off and keeping you here; but I tell you that we have made your fortune. After all," he went on, seeing the other made no sign, "you are doing no worse now than you did a few years ago."

He lit a cigar and paced the room leisurely, like a man who had plenty of time for reminiscences.

"Six years ago," he repeated thoughtfully; "they tell me you were one of the cleverest banknote engravers in Austria; that you could carry a design in your head and could put every line of an intricate design on paper – from memory… It was a hundred-kroner note you tried your hand with, was it not, Maple?" He asked the question carelessly, and Tom Maple shivered.

"The Government just fired you," Helder went on; "it did not want the scandal which a prosecution would have produced. And then you went into the French mint. Somebody recognized you there and you moved on. Where did Gold meet you?" he asked suddenly.

The man in the chair preserved a sullen silence.

"I suppose," Helder continued, "it was on the principle of 'set a thief to catch a thief' that the wily Gold smelt you out. Set a forger to detect a forger, eh?"

He laughed, and Maple looked up, his lips parted, showing his irregular teeth in an ugly grimace.

"Don't laugh, my friend," he said. His voice was shaky. "You talk about a time when I had no responsibilities; I have got one now. I'm a criminal because I am" – his voice sank, he hesitated, then he flung up his head – "a drunkard, and you have played upon my vice. I know you," he nodded his head slowly but menacingly at the other; "I know myself."

His head sunk on his breast. His hands were thrust deep into his pockets. He relapsed suddenly into silence.

Helder and Tiger Brown exchanged a swift glance. As if by mutual impulse they looked at Clinker, but he shook his head in answer to some unspoken question.

"Come, come," said Helder ingratiatingly; "let us have a drink together and talk things over."

The other rose to his feet, shakily supporting himself with his hands on the table. Something had come to him, Helder observed, a dignity which he did not remember ever having seen before. Pitiable figure as he made, there was an unsuspected strength in his attitude.

"I will have no drink," he said quietly; "you don't know what that means to me. Drink has become part of my life, as the air is to you, as the water is to fishes; but I've given it up, and I'm going to stay sober. I have reached the depths and I have started to climb."

Helder's face went dark.

"You're not going to do what I ask?" he said shortly. "If you climb out of here, you climb into a prison cell. You've gone too far, Maple; we won't have any of that folly. There is no clear road for penitence for you or for me. You're in this thing with us, and you've got to stay in it till we all clear out."

Maple shook his head slowly.

"I say you're in it," Helder repeated; "you've done work for us of your own free will; you've got to work now because I want you to. D'ye think," he sneered, "that I'm going to turn you loose on the world to whine your penitence into the sympathetic ears of a

Scotland Yard detective? I'm not such a fool as that. I value my liberty, my place in society, not a little."

"I'm finished," muttered the other; "finished-finished."

"You're not finished," said Helder, "not by a long way. You've got to get into a normal state, whether it's normal drunk or normal sober. See here," he went on, laying his hand on the other man's shoulder, "suppose it came to light that I was responsible for this flood of forgeries; do you know what it would mean? It would mean a lifetime spent in jail. It would mean that I should pass from the life I now live – a life of amiable men and pretty women and pleasant places – to a life which would be worse than death. And you don't suppose for a minute that I would be content to surrender such an existence, or be content to go to jail in the hope that at the end I might gather the crumbs of life to eke out a miserable old age?"

He laughed; the idea seemed to amuse him in a sinister way.

"No, my friend, when I am detected I die quickly; painfully, perhaps, but the pain will be short enough. If I am prepared to kill myself, I am prepared to kill any man who stands between myself and the successful issue of this adventure. I have forged, lied and stolen, that I may achieve what I have; I am prepared to add murder to that if it need be, you understand?"

Maple looked at him listlessly, shaking his head.

"Do you understand?" repeated Helder. "If it becomes necessary I will kill you. I will shoot you like a dog before I shoot myself. You've got to get busy with those English notes. It has to be done quickly; at present the police are only concerning themselves with the American bills. In a month or so they may detect the French notes we have placed on the market."

A strange light came into Maple's eyes.

"They are on the market, are they?"

He showed a quickening of interest. Helder nodded.

"The first batch has gone. Now," he said, with sudden cheeriness, "let us understand each other, Maple. You are going to do as I ask you?"

Maple shrugged his shoulders with a feeble gesture of despair.

"I suppose so," he said; "I've – I've got responsibilities. I've a niece, Helder, unprovided for, worrying about me, and it rattles me."

Helder hid a smile with his hand. "She is provided for," he said. "I have told you that before."

"But how – how?" demanded the other. "She is not the sort of girl who could accept money sent anonymously."

"She is provided for," said Helder again.

The man called Clinker held up a warning hand, signalling the party to silence.

They stood listening.

"There's somebody coming up the road," he said. "I'll go down and see who it is."

He opened the door, and closed it behind him. They heard the big door of the house opened: there was a pause and it closed again. In a minute Clinker was back with a telegram in his hands.

"There was a telegraph boy," he said. "This is for you."

He handed it to Brown, and Brown opened it and read it.

"What is it?" asked Helder.

"They have arrested Schriener in Paris whilst passing a thousand-franc note," said Tiger Brown, and his voice was unsteady. They stood looking at one another: Brown's face was working convulsively. Helder had turned pale. Clinker was supremely uninterested. He was too old a bird, too philosophical a rascal, to be distressed by threat of danger.

But Maple's face was alive with interest: his dull eyes were shining, his lips moved as though he were speaking.

"Schriener – arrested in Paris?" he said eagerly. "A thousand-franc note – was it one of mine?"

Helder looked at him without speaking and nodded his head surlily.

"Ha!" said Maple, and collapsed into a chair.

Helder and Tiger Brown went speeding back to London with the dawn. They were an uncommunicative couple, neither man given to conversation so far as their illegal business was concerned. Nearing Waltham Cross, Brown spoke unexpectedly:

"I can't make out that Maple."

Helder was at the steering wheel; he looked straight ahead as he spoke.

"I think I can," he said. "He sees our finish, or thinks he does, but – " He said no more.

Tiger waited for him to speak, and since he showed no inclination, made an attempt to discuss the matter which was near to him.

"When you spoke of killing Maple," he said slowly, "I guess you were putting a bluff on him."

"Bluff nothing," said Helder, as he deftly turned the car to avoid a market cart. "I'd kill him or anybody else who I thought would betray me – or anybody else," he repeated with emphasis.

"I see," said Tiger Brown.

No further word was spoken.

Helder dropped his companion in the City and went on to the garage where he kept his car. He handed his machine over to the mechanic and walked to Curzon Street.

The net was closing upon him – he felt it. The Russian in prison, Schriener in the hands of the French police, Maple ripe for rebellion – the signs were unhealthy. He had misjudged Maple; had counted too much upon his craving for liquor. He had kidnapped him with a two-fold purpose, and the results had justified the means. For here was Verity Bell in London and Comstock Bell somewhere in the background hiding for reasons of his own.

In a vague way he felt that the new relationship would be useful if the worst came to the worst.

He walked into his study: there was a pile of correspondence awaiting him, for he was gaining in popularity, and invitations were coming faster than of yore. He winced a little at the thought of what might be if his plans miscarried.

He turned them over quickly, one by one, analysing their contents by handwriting and postmark. At last he stopped: there was a letter in an unfamiliar hand.

He opened it; it was from the editor of the *Post Telegram*.

"Will you come and see us at once?" it read. "There has been a development in the Comstock Bell mystery, and as you have been able to supply us with some valuable information, you may help to elucidate the new development. We have reason to believe that Mrs Comstock Bell is dead."

Helder put the letter down and looked out of the window. He had thought that he could supply a solution to the mystery; now, it would seem, it had gone beyond his depth.

IN A JAIL

A taxi carried him to the office of the paper. The Editor had not arrived, but in anticipation of Helder's coming, the young reporter, Jackson, was waiting.

That cheerful journalist gave Helder a nod and a smile, and ushered him into a waiting-room.

"What has happened?" asked Helder, as soon as he was seated.

"I'm blessed if I know," confessed the other. He strode up and down with his hands in his pockets, frankly baffled.

"You know," he said, "that after Comstock Bell had gone, and Mrs Comstock Bell had made her appearance in so startling a fashion, the whole resources of the paper were employed to discover her whereabouts. Although we received a letter written by Comstock Bell and addressed to us from Lucerne, we know for certain that Comstock Bell has not stayed in that city. We had another letter from Vienna."

"What sort of letter?" asked Helder.

"The usual kind – typewritten, signed with a rubber stamp, and countersigned with the name of his wife. Well, we received this letter. Again it was from a fashionable hotel, and again our correspondent discovered that no such party had been staying at the place. We have been running, as you know, a cautious story concerning this mysterious happening. We have had our best men on the track of the couple without in any way getting up with them. The boat trains have been watched; the cross-Channel steamers also, and practically all over Europe there has been a string of correspondents, men who have an entrée which the ordinary private detective would not possess, and our efforts have been fruitless – until last night."

"What happened then?" asked Helder.

"We employed a man to watch the Boulogne boats, and after the homeward-bound boat had left, he went for a little relaxation to the Casino. On the way he overtook a lady who was evidently in a hurry. She was going in his direction, and he thought that it was probable she, too, was going to the Casino. He took very little notice of her, till he saw that she was not turning into the place. He looked round in some surprise when he found she did not follow him, and by the light of the portico he recognized the woman he was sent to watch.

"She hurried on, and took a short cut to the wooden jetty which runs to the sea.

"He hesitated for some time as the whether he should follow her or not; but he knew she must come back the way she went. So he was content to wait on the shore end of the jetty.

"He watched there for two or three hours, and as she showed no signs of returning, walked along till he came to the signal station. To his surprise she had disappeared. He was alone on the pier," said Jackson impressively, and paused to watch the effect of his words.

Helder nodded slowly.

"And?" he said.

"This morning," Jackson went on, "we received a letter from Boulogne. It was signed by Comstock Bell and the girl, and was a protest against the continuance of what they termed 'our persecution.' Here is the letter."

He handed a paper to the other. Helder did not trouble to examine it; with a little nod he handed it back.

"I think I understand," he said. "Was anything seen of Comstock Bell?"

"Nothing whatever. Our theory about the girl is that she is drowned," said the reporter. "It was a fairly rough night, and there was no other way of returning safe by the jetty where our man stood."

Helder rose and looked out of the window.

"Could you do me a favour?" he asked.

"Anything in reason," said the other with a smile. "We can do most things."

"Some weeks ago," Helder said slowly, "a Russian was arrested and charged with being a suspected person."

"I remember the case," said Jackson; "he went to prison for three months and was marked for deportation."

"That is so," said the other quietly. "Now I think if I could see that man there is a possibility of my solving the mystery of Mrs Comstock Bell. Do you think you could get an order from the Home Secretary?"

Jackson pursed his lips dubiously.

"I doubt whether we could," he said. "At any rate, I can try; as soon as the chief comes in we'll see what can be done."

After a few words Helder left. He returned to his flat in Curzon Street. Gold was not in town, he learnt by telephone.

"So much the better," said Helder to himself, "I think that, if I am left alone, I can get myself out of a very bad hole."

With which reflection he went to his room and snatched the few hours' sleep which was so badly needed.

He was awakened at five o'clock in the afternoon by his man, who brought him a telegram. It was from the paper, and read:

"Interview arranged: your Russian is in Chelmsford Gaol. Come office for Home Secretary's order."

Jackson had gone by the time he reached the newspaper office, but the editor was there to see him, and he handed him the authority, motioning him to a seat.

"I am not a curious man," said the editor; "but I am piqued into speculating as to what is the object of your visit to this prisoner. Do you connect Comstock Bell with those wholesale forgeries?"

Helder nodded gravely.

"I do," he said.

In a few word he told the story of the *Cercle du Crime*, and of Comstock Bell's association with that club.

"H'm," said the editor, when he had finished, "I'd heard about it. It seems a pretty average kind of folly; I have known young people do things almost as foolish and more criminal. You say that the man Willetts was betrayed by Bell?"

"I know it," said the other. "Willetts was deliberately and traitorously handed over to the police by Bell to save himself."

"What is your theory about his present disappearance?" the editor asked, eyeing him keenly.

Helder hesitated. Though this matter had been in his mind day and night for months, he had not, strange as it may seem, formulated any scheme by which he might throw suspicion on Bell. It was easy enough to cite the disappearance of the American, and by shake of head, hint, and innuendo, suggest his association with the unknown criminals. It was another matter to give chapter and verse.

"I can say nothing at present," he said. "My own view is that he married this girl because he needed a tool whose mouth would be closed against him in the event of his detection. I believe that at the present moment he is engaged in a last despairing attempt – "

"Excuse me!" the editor interrupted him; "but we know that Comstock Bell is a rich man."

A practical, sober man, this editor, with little romance in his composition, and with a keen appreciation of possibilities.

"He was not only rich before, but he is richer now."

"Now!" repeated Helder wonderingly.

The editor nodded.

"Yes," he said. "His mother, who had been in delicate health for some time, died last week. There was a paragraph about it in most of the papers. She left him the whole of her private fortune. He was already rich; he must be almost a millionaire now. It's a curious business," he said, "without any motive."

"There was no motive for this extraordinary marriage," said Helder quickly.

"There is always a motive for marriage," the editor said tersely.

"If we were to seek for adequate reasons why A marries B we should fill this paper with more mysteries in one day than the average journal will contain in a year. I repeat, there is no motive, no reason in the world why Comstock Bell should be engaged in forgeries.

However," he smiled and held out his hand, "your Russian may tell you things. Good bye."

Helder spent the evening at a theatre. He left by an early morning train for Chelmsford. At nine o'clock he drove up to the grim building and was ushered in to the Governor's office.

Colonel Speyer, a grey-bearded man, received him.

"You want to see our Russian, do you?" he said. "Oh, yes, he's the only Russian we've got, and he's rather a nuisance. You see, nobody speaks his language, and we have to get a man in two or three times a week to find out if there is anything wrong with him, and to explain the rules of the prison to him."

"Pardon me," said Helder, as the Governor was leading the way out of the office, "how does it come that this man is in a place like Chelmsford? I thought prisons like these were specially reserved for local delinquents?"

"We have all sorts of people here," he replied. "It is one of the prisons in which long-service prisoners serve their probation, before going to Portland or Dartmoor. We have all sorts of fellows here. Perhaps, after you have had your interview with the man – by the way, you speak Russian?" he asked quickly.

Helder nodded, and the Governor looked dubious.

"I suppose I ought to have somebody present who can understand you," he said, and glanced down at the Home Secretary's order; "but I can trust you not to violate the rules," and gave him a brief summary of the things he might not ask and the subjects he might not discuss. He led the way to a bare room, which contained a long deal table, scrubbed to a dazzling whiteness. A few minutes later the Russian entered. He was dressed in the hideous khaki of prison uniform, and his small eyes twinkled pleasantly when he saw his erstwhile employer before him.

He sat at one end of the table, and Helder at the other, and between them sat two warders, unemotional men, apparently bored.

Helder noticed as he spoke that they were both industriously writing whilst the conversation continued. He thought they were probably making up their accounts, and he wondered somewhat as to the interior economy of a prison, what the duties of the warders were, and in what manner they found recreation.

His interview was not a long one: it was long enough for him to warn the Russian as to the necessity for silence. He promised him a handsome competence upon his release. As the talk progressed, he found there was no danger to be apprehended from this man; when he rose, at least that doubt had disappeared from his mind.

He found the Governor outside waiting for him.

"Would you like to see the prison?" asked the authority.

He was very proud of his charge: proud of the discipline, the cleanliness, and the order of the convict establishment.

"I shall be delighted," said Helder.

He had wondered if he would have any difficulty in securing the permission which was so readily granted. He followed the Governor through the great hall, where tier after tier of cells rose from the ground to the glass roof. Polished steel balconies ran round three sides of the building, and between each floor a great wire net was stretched.

"We had to have that," said the Governor. "There were one or two attempts at suicide recently."

He was shown into a cell; the door was, at his request, closed on him. He had a morbid desire to realize what imprisonment meant, but he was glad to hear the snick of the lock when the door was opened again.

"The prisoners are exercising," said the Governor. He led the way through into a yard; showed him the tragic little execution shed, the graves of murderers under the wall, their initials chiselled in stone marking their resting place.

A batch of prisoners were at exercise, marching round three flagged circles. Helder watched them as they passed. They were old and young; some of them, indifferent to his scrutiny, returning his glance insolently. Others there were who half turned their heads as they came abreast of him; one such was a tall man, taller by far than any who walked in the rings. Something about his stride was strangely familiar to Helder, and he watched him, he watched his back, kept his eyes fixed on him as he swung round in a circle and again approached; then he strangled the exclamation which rose to his lips, for he had seen the man's face.

It was Comstock Bell!

"What is the matter?" asked the Governor quickly.

"That man – that tall man, who is he?"

"That," said the Governor, "that is Willetts, the forger!"

THE WRITING ON THE BILL

Helder went back to London, his head in a whirl. He had often suspected Comstock Bell's secret, now he had no difficulty in filling in gaps.

Comstock Bell and Willetts were one and the same. Willetts was probably dead, and to avoid scandal Bell had assumed his name and lived a double life, and had voluntarily surrendered himself to punishment under his assumed name.

It explained many things that previously had been inexplicable. Comstock Bell had used his influence to secure the absence from England of both Gold and himself during the trial. That was apparent now.

A sudden thought made him frown. Comstock Bell knew enough to pull the strings in America, he knew the full measure of Helder's guilt. If it meant anything, it meant that the days of the international forgers were numbered. Willetts had been sentenced to twelve months' imprisonment; under the system which existed he would only serve nine months of that sentence, and would then be released. And Comstock Bell released was the greatest danger confronting the forgers.

A wire brought Tiger Brown to Curzon Street, and in as few words as possible Helder explained the situation.

"Now we know why Comstock Bell married," he said, "the mystery of the bandaged hand is a mystery no longer. Comstock Bell suddenly stopped writing letters and took to the typewriter, so that an agent could carry on his correspondence during his absence. He had to find an agent who could be trusted; he married Verity Maple with that object, and it is Verity Maple who had been writing the letters from various parts of Europe, making flying journeys to this place and that, possibly spending only a few hours in a hotel, lunching and seizing the opportunity to take away with her a sheet or two of the hotel stationery."

"'It seems pretty woolly to me," said Tiger Brown. He was not a man of any great imagination. "Why should Bell volunteer for jail? That is the sort of foolishness that gets me."

Helder did not reply immediately. He understood better than his confederate the terrible tyranny of a conscience. He knew the fear that pursues and never relinquishes, that haunting dread of detection which drives sensitive men mad and weak men to drink.

And then there was Comstock Bell's mother. Helder knew something of the invalid woman in New England, proud of her son, and inordinately proud of the honour of her house. She was the determining factor, he was certain.

"It does not seem foolish to me," he said slowly. "We have got to make capital out of this, Tiger; we've two powerful weapons in our hands."

"They are?" questioned the other.

"We know Bell's secret; we hold Tom Maple. We have a league against husband and wife, and it's up to us to use our fortune to the best advantage."

He had, indeed, two powerful levers. Whilst Comstock Bell was in prison, he had, moreover, a certain amount of liberty. He could move freely without any fear that Comstock Bell would put his knowledge to use to his discomfort.

There remained Gold. Helder made a mistake about Gold. Familiarity with the little man had bred contempt for his ability. He underestimated him. This was not to be wondered at, because Gold had not shown the superlative qualities of the ideal detective. Twice Helder had come into conflict with him, and twice the detective had been easily worsted.

He was in no sense apprehensive two days later when he received a polite note from the Embassy detective asking him to call at the Savoy. Gold had returned to London, so the note said, and when Helder reached the self-contained little suite, Gold's baggage was still in the hall with Paris labels fresh upon it.

The detective looked up as the other entered.

"Sit down, will you, Helder?" he said.

He himself rose, went to the door, closed it and remained standing throughout the interview.

He seemed at a loss for an opening. Ever a sign of weakness, thought Helder, watching with amusement the embarrassment of the other.

"I've asked you to call," Gold began slowly, "and I'm going to be frank with you."

"When a man says he's going to be frank," said his guest calmly, "it means he is going to be offensive."

Gold nodded.

"I am going to be offensive," he said: "but you've got to hear me through."

He walked up and down the little apartment speaking jerkily.

"For twelve months," he said, "I have been on the track of the band of forgers who have been circulating spurious currency."

"That much I have gathered," said the other dryly; "you have also done me the honour to suggest that I am not without some guilty knowledge in respect of those forgers."

"I have done more than suggest," said Gold coldly; "I have accused." He looked at the smiling man lying back in the lounge chair. "I know," he said, "that you are in this; I know, too, that in your recent exploits in the realms of high finance," he smiled crookedly, "you have had the assistance of Tom Maple."

Gold was going too near the truth for Helder's comfort. Nevertheless, he made a fine show of indifference.

"You amuse me," he said.

"Maple," continued Gold, "forged the French money. I have proof of this. I have brought you here, Helder, to tell you that either you go

142

right out of this business and quick, or there's going to be the biggest Anglo-American scandal that this little village has ever known."

Helder laughed.

"I would like to humour you," he said pleasantly. "If I possessed sufficient histrionic ability I would fall on my knees before you and confess my gilt, and place myself over in the hands of the prosecution. I would like to do this," he drawled: "I feel that it would be consistent with the spirit of melodrama in which your investigations are being made."

He rose and took up his hat and gloves.

"Unfortunately," he went on, "I cannot oblige you. You have made the most outrageous charges against me," he waved his hand with a fine show of indifference; "I can afford to ignore that. I realize that you're a little baffled, naturally," he said in a mingled tone of sympathy and patronage. "Your work is to find out the criminal and, failing that, you have got to put up some sort of bluff, to tell some probable story. I know I'm not *persona grata* with your boss, and I suppose he will easily swallow the story that, so far from being a fairly innocent broker, I am the bold, bad leader of an international gang of forgers." He laughed again. "A very fine story," he said; "you ought to have written books, Gold; you know as well as I that Comstock Bell is the villain of the piece."

There had come a soft knock on the door. Neither man noticed it. Gold was too intent upon watching the other. The detective was not angry, not even annoyed. He was keenly enjoying the study of this man, who he had no doubt was a criminal and who could, in the face of such deadly peril, assume so nonchalant an attitude.

"Comstock Bell," Helder went on, "is the forger, as you know."

"I would as soon say that Cornelius Helder was an outrageous liar," said a pleasant voice behind him.

The men turned. A woman stood in the doorway, tall and graceful, perfectly gowned. Her presence brought a faint aroma into the smoking-room, the scarcely definable fragrance of rare old flowers.

Helder's face went dusky red, but he did not drop his insolent gaze before the laughing grey eyes of the woman into the doorway.

143

"May I sit down?" she asked languidly.

Gold brought forward a chair and closed the door behind her.

"I am sorry," she said, "I have interrupted a character sketch at its most interesting stage."

She took from her gold bag a little green bottle of smelling salts and sniffed it languidly.

There was an ugly smile on Helder's face.

"I can quite understand your point of view, Mrs Granger Collak," he said. "I might suggest that it is not customary in good society to give a man the lie to his face, though," he smiled again, "it is such a long time since you were — shall I say in the swim — ?"

Gold started then, having little fear but that Mrs Granger Collak could hold her own against the man. He decided to let her deal with him as she thought best. Her advent was unexpected; he had had a vague idea that she was in France. He wondered what business had brought her to him.

"Yes," said the woman sweetly, "it is quite a long time since I was — in the swim. You were still paddling on the edge in those days," she smiled; "but I was 'in the swim,' as you so well express it, long enough to know Comstock Bell, and I know him for a very charming gentleman, the soul of honour, a generous man."

"I do not question his generosity," said Helder significantly; "perhaps you are in a better position to speak on that point than I."

There was no mistaking his meaning.

Mrs Granger Collak took a gold case from her bag, opened it and lit the cigarette she extracted. She lay back in her chair, watching the other with half-closed smiling eyes.

"Yes," she said, as she flicked the match into the fire, "Mr Comstock Bell has been very generous to me, most generous in his judgement."

"The soul of honour, I think, was your phrase?" said Helder.

She inclined her head. "That was my phrase," she said calmly.

"I suppose, Mrs Granger Collak, you are almost an authority on what constitutes honourable dealings?"

"Quite," she said, "I have had to deal with dishonourable people and myself have done dishonourable things. That is what you mean, is it not?"

She smiled again, and he was nonplussed by the directness of the attack.

"But I have never traduced man or woman, lied about them, or sought to injure them."

"That I know," said Helder, with mock humility; "rumour credits you with being – shall I say, kind?"

"You may say what you wish; I only repeat that the man or woman who accuses Comstock Bell of being a forger is either a great fool or a great liar," she added pointedly.

She stopped suddenly and frowned. "I wonder," she said, looking at Gold. She took from her bag a purse, and from that a newspaper cutting, which she handed him without a word.

"Did you insert this?" she asked; "it was about this that I came to see you."

Gold nodded.

"It is very curious that I should have seen it," she said. "it was in an Italian paper. Most of us want thousand-franc notes," she smiled; "but we do not advertise for them."

It was now Helder's turn to sit forward. Who had advertised for a thousand-franc note? Gold would have willingly dispensed with his presence, but it was too late now.

"May I see that cutting?" Helder asked quickly.

Gold handed him the slip of paper. It was in Italian and English, and French and asked that the holders of the thousand-franc bank-notes numbered 687642-687653 should communicate with the French police or with Wentworth Gold.

Helder read it with gathering apprehension.

He did not understand it. There was something ominous in that announcement.

"What are the particular qualities of these notes?" he asked.

Mrs Granger Collak ignored him. From the open purse she extracted a folded banknote, and handed it to Gold.

"Here is one," she said. "I found it amongst my belongings; is it genuine?"

Gold took it, and with his forefinger and thumb snapped it scientifically. He turned it over and looked at the back.

"I am sorry to say this is a forgery," he said; "but I am willing to refund you its face value."

He tried to speak steadily, but his voice was shaking with excitement.

Helder, watching him, grew more alarmed. He guessed rather than knew that this was one of the forged banknotes he had put in circulation, but in what manner did one differ from another? There were two thousand of these notes in circulation somewhere. He knew Gold well enough to understand that, whatever the secret was, it would not be revealed to him. He was too intent upon the problem to desire an further exchanges with Mrs Granger Collak, and he rose from the chair into which he had sunk when Mr Granger Collak had seated herself, and gathered up his hat and gloves.

"I will see you again on that matter, Gold," he said.

The detective nodded brusquely. There was a light of triumph in his eye; he was more cheerful than Helder ever remembered having seen him.

"Goodbye, Mrs Granger Collak," he said, and offered his hand.

She looked at him with that tantalizing smile of hers, but did not take it.

"Goodbye," she said, "you must come and see me — when I am 'in the swim' again."

"Must I wait so long?" he asked. It was a crude rejoinder, and he knew it, but he could think of nothing better to say.

"Now, Tiger, I want you to favour me with your memory," said Helder.

He and his assistant had met in Hyde Park. They were walking slowly in the direction of Kensington Gardens, where the loungers are few.

"I want you," continued Helder, "to remember the circumstances in which those French notes were printed."

"I remember that all right," said Tiger, and gave him a perfect account of the circumstances, so many on one day and so many on another.

"Did any other person handle them but yourself?"

Tiger shook his head

"I took them straight from the machine," he said, "and sent them away."

"Could anybody have got at them?"

"No, impossible."

"No other person touched any of them," persisted Helder.

Tiger Brown hesitated. "Except," he said, "a few that I took to Maple. Don't you remember, he asked to be allowed to see them after they were printed, in order that he might test the ink?"

"I see," said Helder thoughtfully. "So he had some, did he? Was he left alone with them?"

"Yes, he was left to carry out his tests."

"They were collected afterwards?"

"Yes, I collected them myself and they were put into circulation. In fact, to make absolutely sure, they were the notes which I sent out with the first consignment; for I thought if they had passed Maple's test they would pass anything."

"How many notes were there?" asked Helder suddenly.

"Twelve," said the other.

Helder uttered an oath. "The same number of notes that are being advertised for," he muttered; "if Maple has played any tricks on us, by God – " He did not finish.

If trick it was, what could it be? He thought deeply. There must be some explanation for Gold's joy at receiving the note. Gold had behaved like a man into whose hands had been placed the key of the situation. And in all probability each of those banknotes for which he had advertised contained the key.

Sitting down at his desk, he wrote very quickly a dozen wires. They were addressed to various parts of the Continent and to America, and were in code, the simple code which the forger's syndicate employed. When he had finished, he handed them to Tiger Brown.

"Get them away at once," he instructed, "and meet me in an hour's time. I will pick you up outside the Manor House entrance to Finsbury Park."

At the appointed time his big car drew up at the park gates, and Brown sprang in. It was dark by the time they reached the private road which led to the farm.

Gold, left alone with Mrs Granger Collak, had lost no time. He told her in a few words the story of Comstock Bell's disappearance. She had heard about it, all Europe had; but she did not know that an attempt was being made to associate him with the forgeries.

Gold made few mistakes when dealing with individuals. He knew he could trust this woman of whose loyalty to Comstock Bell he was assured. He smoothed the notes on the table before him, and lit a little gas stove. Then he rang the bell. When his man appeared he ordered him to bring a jug of milk. After the man had gone Gold took a little reading-glass and showed Mrs Granger Collak the minute writing on the back of the note. She read it.

"Milk?" she said, bewildered. "What has milk to do with it?"

"I think I understand," said Gold.

He took the jug, laid the note in a saucer, and covered it with the white fluid. Then he lifted it out, shaking off the superfluous drops which clung to it, and held it before the gas-fire to dry.

She sat in silence watching him, and at last he stood up, the note in the palm of his hand. His eyes shone with excitement.

"Well" she said.

Written across the back of the note was line after line of writing, which the milk and heat had revealed.

They read the message together, then Gold reached for his telephone.

"It is very simple," he said, as they stood downstairs waiting for the car which would bring the Scotland Yard men. "It is a well-known kind of secret writing. Moisten the pen with your lips, write your message; it will be invisible till milk and warmth reveal it. I present you with that trick."

Helder had reached the farm and knocked. As a rule the door opened quickly, but on this occasion there was some delay before the sound of bolts rattling their sockets indicated life on the inside of the depressing door. It opened cautiously and Helder slipped in.

The man Clinker explained the delay.

"Maple's ill," he said laconically.

"He'll be worse before I've finished with him," said Helder.

He made his way straight to the strong-room. Maple was lying on the bed, half dressed. His face was white and drawn, his eyes sunken, his lips tinted an unhealthy blue. He opened his eyes as Helder entered but did not address him.

Glowering down on the sick man, Helder realized that he had not a long time to live.

"How long has he been like this?" he asked.

"Yesterday," said the man. "They always go like this if they're used to hard drinking and stop suddenly."

Helder sat on the side of the bed, his hands in his pockets, his head bent forward as he looked from under his eyebrows at the dying man.

"Maple," he said brusquely, "do you remember that batch of French notes that were given to you?"

Maple's head moved feebly.

"You do?" said Helder. "What did you do to those notes?"

Maple closed his eyes with a weary gesture as though the subject had no further interest for him.

"What did you do with them?" repeated Helder. "Speak!"

He grasped the bony shoulder of the sick man and shook him savagely.

"I have got to know, d'ye hear," he hissed. "I've got to know how I stand. What did you do to those notes?"

Tom Maple's lips formed the word "Nothing," but the set of his jaw showed Helder that this was a last act of defiance.

"What did you do with them?" he persisted. "Do you hear, Maple, what did you do with them? I tell you I'm not going to leave you until you answer me. You monkeyed with those bills."

Again he shook the man with all his strength. His teeth chattered and in very weakness the tears rolled down his cheeks, but, dying as he was, he clenched his jaw tighter.

"I –" began Helder, white with rage; then Tiger Brown, a silent spectator of the scene, grasped his arm.

"There's a car coming down the drive," he whispered.

They listened. They could hear the "chuff-chuff" of the engine.

"Get downstairs, get downstairs quickly?" said Brown.

Closing the door of the sick man's room behind them, they made their way to the high-ceilinged living-room and crept to the door. They heard the car stop. Somebody approached the door and knocked, loudly and authoritatively.

Helder laid his finger on his lips to enjoin silence. Again there came a knock, and the three men in the room looked at one another.

Then a deep, clear voice spoke on the other side of the door.

"Open – in the King's name!" it said.

Brown's face went livid.

"The police!" he gasped, and looked round for some way of escape.

Helder did not lose his nerve. The car had been housed in a little shed at the rear of the building. He led the way swiftly across the tiled floor of the kitchen to the rear of the premises. He took a cautious survey from the bay window. There was nobody in sight. He unbolted the door and stepped out, the two men following. They gained the shed.

"Jump in!" said Helder.

He knew the noise of the engines would attract the police, but that had to be risked.

He slipped a big silk handkerchief from his pocket, and tied it round his face, so that only the space between his hat and his eyes was visible.

The car jerked forward over the uneven surface of the yard and gained the road. He saw two men running out from the house, but he had the start, and unless the road was guarded at the other end he would have no difficulty in reaching London. He did not doubt but that sufficient evidence existed to identify him with the gang, but he was playing his last desperate card, and fortune was with him to an extraordinary extent.

WILLETTS

Gold had seen the car vanish. He had not had time to elaborate preparations which would preclude all chances of Helder's escape.

"He can wait," he said, and addressed himself to the task of entering the building.

While he was examining the front door, he realized that the fugitives must have left some other ingress open, and he and the two Scotland Yard men made their way to the back of the building. The door through which Helder had passed was ajar; Gold ran in. The simple arrangement of the interior made a search no difficult matter. The door of Maple's prison had not been secured, and Gold made his way to the bedside of the forger.

It did not need a medical training to know that Tom Maple was in a bad way, and Gold's first business was to send for a doctor. The sick man lay tossing to and fro on his pillow, muttering incoherently. Gold made a quick search of the apartment. He found a number of unfinished plates, damning evidence of the use to which the house had been put. He had finished his search when the detective he had despatched returned with the doctor.

"I'm afraid we shan't be able to get him away," said the surgeon after a brief examination; "his heart is all wrong, and there are probably other complications which I am not now able to discover."

Gold looked at his watch.

"I'm expecting his niece," he said; "I left word for her. By luck I got into communication just before I left town and I wired her to come here. Where is the nearest post office?"

"There is one at Royston," said the doctor; "your car will get you there in twenty minutes."

There was no time to be lost; he must communicate at once with the police and secure the arrest of Helder. He had sufficient evidence now.

He sat down to a little table in the room below, and wrote rapidly. He was in the midst of his message when one of the detectives came in.

"It's Mrs Bell, I expect," said Gold.

He left the half-written message on the table and went out; but it was a man who sprang from the car, a tall man, whose walk was strangely familiar to Gold.

"Bell!" he gasped.

Without a word Comstock Bell strode into the house. In the light thrown by a hanging lamp his face was pale and drawn.

"Where's my wife?" he asked.

"I'm expecting her," said Gold, in surprise.

A shadow of alarm passed over the young man's face.

"Where have you – ?" began Gold.

"I will tell you later," said the other hurriedly. "I passed my wife's car four miles on the road; it had broken down and the chauffeur told me she must have gone on here. Could she have missed the way?"

Gold shook his head.

"I don't think it's possible. She may have gone back to London. I will send this message off by one of the men and go back to town with you in your car."

"Where's Maple?" asked Comstock Bell.

"He's upstairs," answered the other gravely.

"Is he dead?" Comstock Bell's voice was sharp, his face went suddenly hard.

"No, he's not dead," said Gold; "but I'm afraid he won't last long."

"Is he conscious?"

The doctor was coming downstairs as he spoke, and overheard the question.

"He's conscious now," he said; "but he ought not be worried."

Comstock Bell hesitated.

"This is a matter which affects my whole life," he said. "Suppose he were not worried, is it possible to save him?"

The doctor shook his head.

"Then I must speak to him," said Comstock Bell decidedly. "Come with me!"

The three men went upstairs together. Maple lay in his bed, propped up on the pillows. He smiled feebly at Gold, who was the first to enter, but as the tall form of Comstock Bell came through the doorway his eyes widened and his lips trembled in apprehension.

"Comstock Bell?" he whispered.

The other nodded and, walking slowly to the side of the bed, sat down and laid his hands gently on the thin wrists of the other.

"Where have you come from?" he asked Maple in a weak voice.

Comstock Bell hesitated, then he said slowly:

"I have just come form prison."

"Prison?" whispered the other.

Comstock Bell nodded. There was a deathly silence in the room. Gold realized the affairs had reached the great crisis in Comstock Bell's life. He watched the tall young man, his lean face softened with compassion as he leant forward over the bed.

"From prison," he repeated. "Years ago there was a forgery committed in Paris. Two students were involved, one committed the forgery and passed the note, the other was unaware that his friend had taken such a desperate step. They had discussed the forgery as a great joke; both were known to be concerned in the plot, and when the crime was detected both men left the country. For some time their identities were confused."

Tom Maple lay staring at the ceiling, his lips framing the words he could not speak.

"A few months ago," Comstock Bell went on, "I, who was the innocent member of the little confederacy, gave myself up to the police for the crime, because I was sick with apprehension, and because I knew that the police were again searching for Willetts. In Willetts' name I was condemned and sentenced."

"And Willetts is dead," said Gold. "Why did you do such a mad thing?"

"Willetts is alive," said Comstock Bell.

The man on the bed smiled faintly.

"Yes," he said in a low voice, "he is alive – I am Willetts."

He turned over on his side and continued as though speaking to himself; they had some difficulty in hearing him, for at times his voice sank till it was but a whisper.

"I am Willetts," he went on, "poor Tom Willetts; Willetts," he whispered wonderingly, "I thought I should never hear that name again."

He was silent for a long time, so long that they thought he had fallen asleep, and the doctor leant over him, touching his face gently.

"He is dead," said the doctor.

An hour later Comstock Bell and Gold were on their way to London. There were mutual explanations.

"I left Chelmsford this morning," said Comstock Bell. "I received the remission of my sentence as a result of the action of the French police – it was Lecomte's doing, and I went straight on to Southend, which my wife had made her headquarters."

Gold was a little puzzled and showed it, and Comstock Bell explained briefly.

"When I had decided that I should expiate the crime of which I was accused, I looked about for an agent who I could trust. I decided to marry. My plan was to keep my imprisonment secret. To this end I bought a tug-boat and had it fitted. My object was to allow my agent to pass unobserved to and from London, which was necessary for many reasons. The day I left England on my honeymoon I went no farther than Boulogne; my tug carried me back to a seaside resort, and from thence my wife and I journeyed to London. That night I surrendered. By a piece of ill-fortune my wife was seen at my house. She had gone there to find a rubber stamp with my name which I had foolishly left behind."

"I understand now," said Gold. Rapidly he reviewed the details of Verity Bell's reappearance in the light of her husband's explanation.

"The day of my release was made know to my wife," Comstock Bell went on, "and it was arranged that she should wait for me at Southend. You knew she was there?"

Gold nodded.

"I knew she was there; I did not know it was her headquarters."

"To my surprise," said Comstock Bell, "she was not awaiting me. It was there I found your wire telling her to go to the house on the Cambridge Road."

"There is only one thing to do," said Gold, "you can safely leave the London end to the police; let us get back to your tug; your wife may have returned."

Comstock Bell hesitated.

"She may have gone back to see you," he said.

"In that case she is safe," said Gold. "Fortunately, we have not gone far out of our way; we can turn off at the next village. From this side of Waltham Cross there is a direct road to Southend."

They had no difficulty in finding the way. The tug was moored some distance from the shore, and at that time of night it would have been no easy task to find a waterman to row them out. But near the pierhead, Lauder, the skipper of the tug, was waiting for them.

His news was not reassuring. Mrs Comstock Bell had not returned.

"But if you come to the tug, sir, he said, "I think I have information for you which will be helpful."

They rowed out to the *Seabreaker*.

"It's about this Mr Helder," said the skipper. "I have an idea that he may have something to do with the lady's disappearance."

They were seated in the little saloon, which bore traces of a woman's hand, for these two saloons had been Mrs Comstock Bell's home.

"Going up and down the river as I have been doing frequently," said the skipper, "there's very little in the way of new buildings which have escaped me. Three months ago a new boat-house was built on the Essex shore, between Tilbury and Barking. I thought it was a rum place for a pleasure craft."

"A pleasure craft?" said Gold quickly.

The skipper nodded.

"Yes," he said, "one of the finest motor-boats I have ever seen, and a sea-going one at that. I saw the makers doing their trials. Since then she has been on the slips and not once have I seen her in the water. Every day a man comes to look her over, and from what my son picked up from the attendant, one day when we were lying off the boat-house, waiting for your lady, she's got spirit and provision enough to take her a ten days' voyage."

"It's strange," said Gold.

He looked at Comstock Bell and saw that the young man was impressed.

"After all," Gold went on thoughtfully, "it's a way out of London which Helder would think of; it would be worth the money in case of emergency, and likely as not Helder will try it."

"I think it is Mr Helder," put in Lauder; "at any rate, the man who looked after the boat told my boy it was an American gentleman."

"The best thing we can do," said Comstock Bell, "is to go up the river to this mysterious boat-house. We can lose nothing. We can spare a man to watch it if the boat has not gone and can resume our journey to London."

Gold nodded, and the Captain went forth to his little bridge. In a few minutes the *Seabreaker* was under way, steaming up the river against the tide. The night was a dark one; they passed three big steamers coming down on the ebb. There was no sign of the motor-boat till they had left Tilbury behind.

Then Lauder's voice rang out sharply, and suddenly the tug listed to starboard as she swung round.

"There goes something!" shouted the captain from the bridge.

Abreast of them and running at full speed, her engines buzzing noisily, a long, lean motor-boat slipped past, between the tug and the Essex shore.

Her little aft cabin was ablaze with lights, and then of a sudden these were extinguished.

"She's going a bit too fast for me," said the captain; "but I'll overtake her when she reaches rough water."

Bell strained his eyes towards the little black hull. Dark as it was, the foam of her wake was visible. The tug's engines were now spinning at full speed and the distance between the two vessels was maintained.

"It may not be her," said Gold; "but we must risk that. It is certainly a mysterious craft which tries to slip from the Thames with her lights out."

In the darkness the skipper grinned.

"I have done the same pretty often recently," he said.

"I think – " said Comstock Bell; then suddenly across the water from the boat ahead came a shrill scream, then another.

The cabin of the boat was suddenly illuminated and silhouetted between the light and the watchers were two figures standing on the stern of the boat.

Comstock Bell clearly saw a man and a woman. In a moment they parted as one slipped from the boat into the dark water.

"It is the woman!" he whispered hoarsely.

HELDER SLIPS TO SEA

In a deserted part of the Cambridge road, Helder, flying from justice, had come upon a car which had broken down. It lay in such a position that it was necessary to slow down to pass it.

A woman sat on the bank reading. The chauffeur had apparently gone to the nearest town for assistance.

Even in that moment of peril Helder was not so engrossed that he could pass any woman without the scrutiny which was habitual in him. She raised her head as the car came abreast; Helder's foot went to the brake and the machine stopped with a jar.

"Mrs Comstock Bell, I believe?" he said.

She faced him fearlessly, complete mistress of herself though not of the situation, for Helder was a primitive man in such moments as these.

"I shall trouble you to come along with me," he said.

She made no reply; she knew it was useless to argue with the man, but she threw a quick glance along the darkening road. There was nobody in sight and she realized her danger.

Helder stepped aside and opened the door of the tonneau invitingly, but there was a threat in the invitation.

"I'm not going," she said resolutely.

She wanted to parley, to gain time; but in that moment of crisis she could think of nothing to say, and Helder was alive to the danger of delay.

"Get in," he said roughly.

She shrank back; he caught her arm and half lifted her into the car.

"If you scream," he said, turning from his driver's seat, "I will kill you, do you understand that? Put up the hood." He addressed Tiger Brown sharply.

They had strapped the hoot taut when the lights of another car came into sight over the crest of the hill, a mile away.

"Get one on each side of her, and hold her hands," said Helder; "if she screams, stop her."

Brown hesitated. There was an ugly look in his face which Helder rightly interpreted. Out of the pocket of his white dust-coat he slipped a revolver.

"You're not going to spoil my game," he said, "d'ye hear? You monkey with me and it's hell for you."

There was something that was almost inhuman in his rage-distorted voice, and Tiger sank down in the seat with a gasp.

They passed the other car at full speed. It was night when they reached London. They slipped through the busy streets ablaze with lights at what seemed to the driver a snail's pace, but which was all too quick for the silent captive. Helder avoided the more populous districts, skirting the suburbs, and bore steadily east till they reached the marshland of Essex, and London was only a glow of warm light in the sky.

Helder had formed his plan as he went. He had made careful preparation for such an emergency. Throughout England, in unlikely places, he had rented or bought cottages. He knew the value of a fixed abode, and the danger which awaited the criminal whose idea of safety lay in moving quickly from place to place.

Ten miles out of Barking there is a deserted stretch of flat country, bordering the river. An insalubrious factory or two, an aviation ground, and the storage wharf of a coal factor completed the habitations on the river front.

It was to the coal wharf that Helder directed his car. He seemed to know the road very well.

"We'll get out here," he said suddenly.

There was no house in sight; they seemed to be the only creatures alive in the damp and dismal neighbourhood. Ahead of them the girl could see the orderly mounds of coal which stood stacked up upon concrete foundations; she guessed rather than saw the wooden fence which marked the limits of the factor's holding. For one wild, frantic moment she feared for her life.

Helder gripped her arm, and half led, half pushed her forward.

"No harm will come to you," he said; "if you are sensible," he added.

They left the factor's store on the left and walked and stumbled forward for a quarter of an hour. In the darkness the girl distinguished a squat building which stood on the edge of the water. The tide was high, and Helder gave a little grunt of satisfaction.

He fumbled for a moment at the door of the building, opened it, and pushed her before him inside.

A faint smell of tar and petrol greeted her.

Helder lit a lamp and she saw that she was in a large boat-house, and in the centre of the well-greased slips was a big motor-boat. The guides sloped down to the big doors at the other end and apparently continued into the water.

Helder watched her as she took in the details.

"This is my lifeboat," he said, with a return to his old good humour – he pointed to the big launch affectionately – "waiting to carry me safely from the wreckage," he said. "I think it is time we left this country."

His two companions were examining the boat with interest.

Tiger Brown, terrified as he was at the prospect, could not withhold his admiration for his employer's foresight.

"Say, she's a dandy!" he said.

"She's provisioned for a long voyage, and she's a good sea boat," Helder remarked.

Suspended from the ceiling was a steel chain from the end of which hung a handle. He pulled this, and the doors at the other end swung open, showing the black waters of the river beyond.

"Get in," he said. He pointed to the ladder leaning against the side of the boat-house, and Brown, planting it firmly against the boat, mounted. Helder turned to the girl.

"I shall not go," she said vehemently. "I don't care what you do, I will not go. Aren't you satisfied with the work you've already done?"

"I think you will go, Mrs Comstock Bell," said Helder deliberately. "I have no desire to meet your husband in Chelmsford Jail."

She went white to the lips and staggered back. Helder laughed.

"Yes, that secret of yours has been very well kept, and, so far, I am the only living person in England except yourself who knows. I don't think it matters one way or the other," he said; "and really I think your husband is supersensitive. But you will save me a lot of trouble and yourself some unpleasantness if you offer no resistance to my plan."

"My husband is an innocent man," said the girl steadily; "he is suffering for another's sin."

Helder bowed politely.

"Most people who inhabit prisons are innocent; they generally suffer for the offences of others," he said. "Get in!" His tone was imperative, brutal. "Get in!" he said again, harshly. "I tell you I want you, you're necessary, and I'm going to take you, if I have –" He ended abruptly.

She knew that resistance was useless. By some means she could not guess, Helder had discovered the secret she had devoted all her care to guarding. To disobey him now would in all probability mean the betrayal of Comstock Bell.

She glanced despairingly at Helder's companions. Brown had shown reluctance to obey, but now with freedom before him, he was as anxious as Helder to be gone. There was only the man Clinker. Yet she saw no look of sympathy in his eyes. Her hand was trembling as she grasped the ladder and mounted to the boat, but she showed no other sign of terror.

Helder followed after her and put the ladder away.

He leant over the stern of the vessel, knocked out the detaining wedge that held the boat, and she slid smoothly down into the water and swung round with the tide. In a minute the engines were revolving noisily and the motor boat was heading down river.

Clinker and Tiger Brown had gone forward, and Helder was left alone with the girl in the little cabin aft. He switched on a small light, evidently fed by an accumulator battery under the seat. She moved nearer the door at the stern.

"Perhaps you can give me some information?" he said, after a while.

She made no reply.

"I think perhaps there is little you can tell me," he went on. "I understand as much about your marriage as you. I'm rather curious to know how your uncle betrayed us."

Her lips were pursed close together; there was look of scorn in her fine eyes which maddened him.

He reached across with one hand, he switched out the light, and with the other caught her roughly by the wrist. With a quick movement she wrenched herself free and sprang to the stern of the little cabin.

"If you come near me," she said, "I will jump overboard."

There was no mistaking the determination in her tone.

"You need not be afraid," he said with a laugh; "you're too valuable an article to be damaged. I suppose Comstock Bell will pay pretty handsomely for you."

As he spoke he edged his way nearer to her, and then, without a moment's warning, sprang at her and caught her in his arms. She shrieked loudly, and in the silence of the night it seemed as though she would arouse all that was alive on the sleeping river.

"Be silent!" he said savagely.

"Let me go!" she cried.

"Will you promise you won't scream?" he said.

"Let me go!" she said again.

He released her and went back to the cabin.

"Come in here," he ordered roughly.

"Put on the light," she said.

He clicked the little button and the cabin was again flooded with light. Still, she did not move, save to turn her head. Then her body grew tense.

"Thank God!" he heard her whisper, "the *Seabreaker*."

He looked aft. Behind them, coming at full speed, was a tug, and in a moment he comprehended its significance.

He sprang forward and put his hand over her mouth and strove to drag her into the cabin. For a moment they struggled, and the little launch rocked to and fro with the violence of their efforts. Then suddenly she wrenched herself free. He put out his hand to catch her, but he was too late; she had dived head first into the water.

He heard the shrill clang of the tug's engines, and knew that there had been witnesses to her act. He took a quick step into the cabin and turned out the lights again.

Tiger Brown came swiftly aft.

"What is the matter?" he said.

Helder made no reply for a moment; then he laughed.

"If we can reach the Belgian shore before daylight," he drawled, "we shall be extremely fortunate."

He looked back. He was rapidly increasing the distance between himself and his pursuer; for the *Seabreaker* had been turned broadside on, and he did not doubt that the boat had been lowered to pick up the girl.

"Somehow" – he was speaking half to himself – "I do not think we shall reach the Continent."

THE IRONY OF CHANCE

In the pretty saloon of the *Seabreaker* Verity Bell lay, weak but smiling; her husband sat by her side.

The tug had turned and was making its slow way upstream, and Gold, by the Captain's side, was silently speculating upon the result of the telegram he had despatched to shore, which, if effective, would place watchers along the French and Belgian coasts awaiting the coming of Helder.

But whatever tragedy awaited the men in the motor-boat, tossed and beaten by the nor'-wester which raged outside, there was something of tragedy in the scene which was being enacted in the little saloon. For here was Comstock Bell, a man vindicated, grateful to the point of worship, and here was his wife, of whom he had no more than twelve hours' knowledge, no nearer to him by conventional standards than any casual acquaintance. She had served her purpose.

This she herself thought, lying there, utterly weary, too exhausted by her recent experiences to do anything but think.

She had served her purpose – and now?

She had looked at him through half-closed eyes for a long time before he realized that she had returned to consciousness; took in the new lines about his mouth which prison life had given him, the spareness – prison diet was responsible – and the new look of content which comes to a man who is free of care and from whose soul has been lifted a weight of secret fear.

She was ready to face the worst, yet having no clear idea in her mind as to what was the best, still less could she decide with any certainty what development she desired least. In this same cabin, on this very settee, she had gone into this very question time and time again with no greater profit. What was her future – and his?

A solution, she had thought, was divorce: yet she shrank from that, and with good reason. For the English law is a beastly law, and denies relief to the decent and clean. You must qualify in the hog trough for divorce, you must strip the fine cloak of modesty, be blatantly unashamed, else you must go on living the life which circumstances have made for you.

With Comstock Bell, the issue was clearer. He had no greater strength of mind than she, yet since he must take the initiative, his plan had been insensibly formed. And it was no factor in his decision that the girl who lay inert upon the settee was beautiful by all tests. Never before had he found time to look at her critically; even now his critical faculties were biased by the knowledge of the great service she had rendered to him by the sacrifice which he felt she had made. He knew instinctively that, however largely his fears had bulked in the affair of the £50 note, however much he may have thought, standing upon the threshold of voluntary immolation, that that period was the turning point of his life, now was the great moment upon which the future depended.

She looked very fragile, he thought. She had changed her wet things into a long silk kimono, dull red, and it threw into contrast the clear whiteness of her skin.

She opened her eyes with a smile.

"Well?" she said.

It was a little friendly monosyllable, but it struck the note he most desired.

"You were surprised to see me, weren't you?"

An unaccountable shyness prevented him calling her by her name.

"No, I was not surprised," he said calmly; "but I am surprised now that I was not."

There was a long silence, which she broke.

"My uncle," she said, "is he – "

Comstock Bell nodded sadly.

"I was afraid so," she said gently. "Poor uncle!"

"He was much too near my own age," she said gently, "for me to regard him as one usually does that sort of relation, but he was very good to me." Her eyes filled with tears. "I am –" She stopped suddenly, and a tinge of red crept into her face.

"What?" he asked in a low voice.

She shook her head.

"Nothing – nothing" she said hastily.

"You were going to say you were alone in the world," said Comstock Bell, gently, and he took one of her listless hands in his; "and yet" he continued with a smile, "you cannot say that any more than I."

He paused a little, then –

"We are married, you know," he said.

There was pain in the eyes which met his.

"I know," she said quickly. "I somehow wish that you hadn't spoken of that," she went on, looking past him; "we ought to face this situation sensibly, oughtn't we?"

He nodded, waiting for her solution.

"You see" – she turned on her side, supporting her head with one hand, and she was very serious – "you see, if this were a story, we ought to live happily ever after – and I want it to end like a story. But it does not mean happiness for either of us – like this. I must not spoil your life – "

"Nor I, yours," he interrupted.

"That doesn't matter so much," she said with a little smile; "my life would have been utterly spoilt if I had refused to help you…and it could only happen as it has happened. You see…" she hesitated; "when you told me your plans and the story of your foolish Crime Club… I knew."

"Knew what?"

"That my uncle was Willetts." She looked into his face gravely.

"Maple is my name and Uncle Tom adopted it…for reasons. I knew that it was my duty to go through the ceremony… I could not tell you that you were innocent, because you knew that already."

"I knew that," he said quietly; "yet I was morally guilty. It was my suggestion the forgery. I made it in jest to Willetts when the club started. We were both keen draughtsmen and in fun I sketched... I never dreamt he would do such a mad thing."

The thud-thud of the tug's screw was the only sound in the cabin.

"We have not disposed of ourselves," said the girl after a while, "and we must be sensible."

"Which means that we have got to do something disagreeable," he smiled; "it would be very easy to say, 'I will leave everything to you,' and pass my responsibility on. You would sacrifice your life − no, no, don't interrupt, Verity − you would offer a way out easy enough for me − but no way out which means the dissolution of our marriage is acceptable."

She flushed.

"It would be wrong to go on with this," she said in a low voice, "in...in the way marriages go on. It would be equally wrong in me if I accepted your name...your fortune − and gave you nothing but the comforting feeling that you had played the game."

She sat up and threw back her hair with a jerk of her head.

"And it would be wrong...because I am a woman capable of loving...no fortune, no honour would compensate...suppose in years to come I learnt to love somebody...?"

She dropped her eyes before his.

"I anticipate that," he said gently. "I think you will learn to love somebody...and that somebody will be me."

She did not speak.

"You have taken one great risk for me," he went on, "will you take another...that when love comes it may be for your husband?"

She raised her head and looked at him long and earnestly. Then she held out her hand.

"I will," she said.

Out on the North Sea the little motor-boat was fighting its way through the storm, which increased in ferocity every moment.

The tiny craft leapt and fell from crest to trough. Helder, in an oilskin coat, the collar turned up to his eyes, stood by the steersman amidships. Tiger Brown, never the man for a rough crossing, lay prostrated in the little cabin below.

"Is it likely to be any worse?" roared Helder above the thunder of the storm.

The steersman shook his head.

"I can't say," he replied; "it looks as though it was going to be a dirty night."

The motor-boat trembled as a wave broke over its bow, and the steersman turned to the man at this side.

"You must get across?" he asked; "we couldn't creep back to some quiet little harbour and lay till the storm passes?"

Helder made no reply. He glanced back. Trembling on the horizon was the yellow glow of the lightship they had passed.

Another wave struck the little craft and it heeled over. He was no sailor, but he knew that this could not go on. Perhaps his going to sea had served a purpose.

"We'll go back," he said. "Where can we run to?"

The man at the wheel thought for a few minutes.

"We could double back into the Thames," he said.

Helder shook his head.

"No," he said, "that would be too dangerous. If the weather would admit of it we could go down the Channel, but that would be almost as dangerous as to attempt to cross, and we have not much time. It will be daylight in four hours."

"Why not make for Clacton?" said the steersman; "there are a dozen lonely places one could land at and escape observation."

"We'll take our chance," said Helder, "put her back. Put into shore now and we'll land wherever seems most likely."

In the lee of the shore the water was smoother, and at four o'clock in the morning the nose of the boat grated against the sands between Clacton and Walton. The little party waded ashore.

"What about the boat?" asked Tiger Brown. He had recovered sufficiently to take an interest in things.

Helder hesitated. He did not want to lose the boat, it represented a last chance of escape. But he knew that it would be discovered in the morning by the coastguards, and the evidence of his being in England would set the police at work with renewed vigour. There was nothing to do but to sacrifice the little craft in which he had placed such reliance. She was turned till her stern touched the sand, the engines set at full speed and the wheel locked. Putting her nose in the direction of the wide sea, the four men released their hold on her and she went buzzing out of sight.

They were wet through, drenched by the spray and their voluntary immersion, for it had been necessary to stand waist high in the water whilst they were preparing the motor-boat for her last trip to sea. The sands were deserted, they met no coastguards. They gained the village of Little Clacton without meeting a soul.

Here they separated; each man had a supply of money.

"Which way do you go?" asked Brown.

"I shall go back to London," said the other. "You had better go – " He hesitated. For the life of him he could not make any suggestion. His own plans were so uncertain, his chance of getting clear so unlikely, and he was, moreover, so absorbed in his own plight that he had little inclination to concern himself with his companion's route.

"Don't worry about me," said Tiger. "I think I shall find a way."

Helder left them in the darkness and went on to Clacton station.

He must take his chance of getting an early train to the Continent. Fortune was with him here, for a freight train was moving slowly out as he came to the goods yard.

He had to climb a fence to reach the prohibited area of the railway.

His clothes were torn, his hands, so unused to manual labour, sore with his efforts.

He stopped by the rail as a long train slowly moved past. He watched his opportunity; a cold storage van came abreast. The centre doors were open, for it was empty; he leapt up, caught a rail and swung himself on to the floor of the van. He sat there, shivering in his wet clothes, planning his next move.

Unless the train was deplorably tardy, he ought to be in Colchester well within an hour. He gathered by the length of the train that it was unlikely to stop at the wayside stations to pick up trucks. In this surmise he was correct. After an unconscionable time the train pulled up before a signal outside Colchester station. He dropped off, made his way across some fields and reached the town safely. He met one or two men on their way to work. He was chilled to the bone and desperate; he would have to run the risk of their talking.

He watched till he saw a man, evidently of a superior class of artisan, coming towards him. The man was walking briskly, and whistling a little tune, when Helder stopped him.

"Excuse me," he said.

The man stopped dead; by the light thrown from a street lamp fifty years away he saw the bedraggled figure and eyed him suspiciously.

"Do you want to earn a fiver?" asked Helder.

"I do," said the man, but without enthusiasm.

"I have had a motor accident," said Helder; "I have had to walk across the country five miles. I want a lodging and a suit of clothes."

The working man detected a note of refinement in the other's tone and was more respectful.

"There are plenty of lodgings," he said, "and you will be able to get some clothes as soon as the shops open."

"I want them now," said Helder, "I don't want to wait. How far do you live from here?"

"About five minutes, but it isn't the sort of place you'd like to go to."

Helder brushed aside his objections.

"I don't want to go to an hotel," he said. "I have reasons" – he suggested one which was more creditable to his powers of imagination then his morals. "I don't want anybody to know I'm down here," he explained, "and any suit of dry clothes will do me."

He took out his pocket-book, selected two five-pound notes, and handed them to the man.

"Come this way, sir," said the workman respectfully.

He led the way to a little street of cheap villas and opened the door. He showed the way into the little parlour and lit a lamp.

"I'll go up and tell the missus," he said, "and see what I can find you."

The chill room felt warm after the draughty interior of a cold-storage van. In a few minutes the man came back bearing a bundle of clothes under his arm and with many apologies laid them out on the small horsehair sofa.

"The missus will be down in a minute," he said "she'll get you some tea."

He went out while Helder changed. It was evident he had brought his best suit, and it was more welcome to Helder than the finest fit at Poole's. It changed his appearance so that, from the fashionably dressed "man about town," he became a commonplace type of workman. He declined the collar the man offered him, but accepted gratefully a woollen scarf. He transferred from the pockets of his old clothes everything that might serve to identify him. When he was dressed, the man's wife, in inelegant *deshabille*, brought him a cup of tea and lit the little fire.

"You understand," said Helder to the man, "that I don't want this matter spoken about. I am supposed to be in London, and it would do me a lot of harm if it were known that I was gallivanting about the country."

The man nodded with a sagacious wink.

"You may trust me," he said with a knowing smile. "What shall I do with the old clothes?"

"Dry them and keep them," said Helder.

He drank the tea and ate the two thick slices of toast the man made for him.

The day was beginning to dawn gradually; he did not wait for broad daylight before he made his way to the station. He took a workman's ticket for Romford, there he bought another ticket for London.

By luck the clerk did not take away the ticket for the first half of his journey. This was all to the good.

It was eight o'clock when he reached Liverpool Street station. The streets were crowded with early workers on their ways to their offices. It was necessary to avoid London as much as possible; he realized this. He made his way eastward, found a ready-made tailor's shop, and bought a heavy overcoat and hat unlike any he had ever worn.

By a circuitous route, which necessitated crossing the river at Woolwich, he reached New Cross, the South Eastern station, where slow trains sometimes stop on their way to the coast.

Here again luck was with him. It was much easier than he had imagined possible. He was tired out from want of sleep and his exertions of the previous night.

He dozed as far as Ashford; here he got out, for there was a five minutes' wait. He had a cold luncheon at the buffet bar and bought a paper.

It was from a bundle which had just been unwrapped and had evidently come by the same train as himself. He opened it and first news he read turned him white.

It was headed: "The International Gang of Forgers: Flight and Return of Helder, the Leader."

He bit his lip to prevent himself uttering an exclamation, and read:

"Scotland Yard has succeeded in tracking down the gang which for years has been manufacturing and putting into circulation forged United States bills. Last night Mr Wentworth Gold, an official attached to the American Embassy, discovered the distributing centre of the gang. It was situated on the Cambridge road, some twenty-five miles out of town. Mr Gold, who was accompanied by a number of Scotland Yard men, arrived too late to capture the leaders, who made their escape in a motor-car.

"It was afterwards discovered that they had reached the Thames in the vicinity of Barking, where a motor-boat was awaiting them. They made for the open sea and soon out-paced their pursuers.

"The torpedo boat flotilla lying in Dover Harbour was communicated with, and immediately put out and made a systematic patrol of the sea to within three miles of the French and Belgian coasts. No sign of the motor-boat was seen, however, and at first it was believed that, owing to the rough weather in the North Sea, the boat was swamped.

"A discovery made this morning upsets this theory and proves without doubt, that, unable to face the terrible weather, the boat put back. The men evidently landed between Clacton and Frinton and, turning the boat's head to the sea, sent her out again at full speed, empty.

"By good fortune it was sighted three miles out by the TBD *Searcher,* and with some difficulty was boarded. With commendable promptitude the officer commanding the torpedo boat destroyer noted the motor boat's course, and putting in to Clacton landed a search party which found traces of the landing. These included a pair of night glasses, evidently the property of Helder.

"So far the men have not been tracked, though the police are working on a clue which they have obtained at Colchester. They have reason to believe that Helder has doubled back to London, with the object of leaving for the Continent by the regular mail service.

"All passenger boats at Dover, Folkestone, Newhaven and Harwich are being carefully watched."

Helder folded the paper carefully, and slipped it into his pocket. To go on now would be disastrous, to go back almost as dangerous.

While he was considering his line of action a Northern-bound train came steaming into the station and pulled up at another platform. His mind was quickly made up. He crossed the bridge and entered the train. He had no time to get a ticket, nor had he any desire to attract attention to himself. He did not doubt that the police would trace him to New Cross, but he would baffle them yet.

If he had hoped to leave the train at a wayside station he was disappointed. From Ashford to London the train ran without a stop, this would bring him into the very heart of London again; he would have to run the gauntlet of the detectives who would be watching at the station. His only hope was that they were confining their attentions to the outward-bound trains. If he had any luck, he would arrive between the hours at which these trains departed.

The train stopped at Waterloo. The inspectors came to collect the tickets. It was the chance he had prayed for. He left the train and walked boldly up to the barrier where the collector stood.

He took a pound-note out of his pocket as he approached the man.

"I had no time to buy a ticket at Ashford," he said.

He did not wait for the change, but pushed on. A foolish proceeding, because he was still wearing the clothes of an artisan. He recognized his mistake before he had reached Waterloo Junction.

Fate was playing with him that day and playing in his favour, for no detective saw him, though, as it happened, there were half a dozen watching Waterloo.

He came by tube across London and reached Highgate. Here he made a number of purchases, including a grip and a change of clothing. With this he doubled back again, using the convenient tube to South London, took another train to Sydenham; and used the opportunity which an empty carriage presented to change his clothes. The others he placed in the grip. His purchases had included a pair of gold spectacles, and the change in his appearance was startling.

In the meantime Gold was hot on his tracks. The ticket-collector at Waterloo had told the story of the man in rough working clothes who had given him a pound note and told him to keep the change.

At five o'clock in the afternoon they arrested Tiger Brown at Brentford. Exactly how he came to Brentford is not of any great importance. He could tell them nothing more than they already knew about Helder. It was almost impossible to follow the latter's movements.

"He has twisted and doubled so about London," said Gold, "that I'm hanged if I know where to look next."

Helder was, in fact, edging by a series of short zigzag tracks farther and farther from the metropolis. He reached Reading by the least likely of railways; he was making for Fishguard and he arrived at the western port in time to catch the Irish boat, but he passed unchallenged.

But Fate, which had favoured him so greatly, now played her most cruel card, and the story of Helder's arrest will go down to history as the most remarkable incidence of poetic justice that has ever been known.

They woke Gold in the early hours of the morning with a telegram which was from the detective in charge of the case. It was brief. "Helder arrested at Queenstown," it said.

Gold caught the early morning train and crossed the Irish Channel that afternoon. He went to the little police station on the quay. Helder was in the cell, nonchalant, almost insolent in his carelessness.

"Well, Gold," he said. "You've got me."

Gold nodded.

"Yes," he said, "you've had a run for your money."

Helder laughed bitterly.

"Did they tell you how I was arrested?" he asked.

"No," said Gold, in some surprise. The incident of the arrest had not been detailed to him, and it struck him as curious that the prisoner should regard the matter as being one worth speaking about.

Helder laughed; his back against the wall, both his thumbs in his waistcoat pockets.

"I went into a tourist's agency to get a ticket to America," he said. "I handed them two five-pound notes. I did not think much of the agent's delay in getting me the ticket. A few minutes later a detective came in and I was arrested."

"They recognized you," said Gold.

The smile on the other's face was tragic.

"No, they did not recognize me," he said slowly. "The two notes I handed over in exchange were forged."

Gold's eyebrows rose.

"But you did not forge five-pound notes," he said.

Helder shook his head.

"That's the cursed joke," he said; "they were somebody else's forgeries that had been passed on to me."

THE END

Mrs Comstock Bell sat at breakfast on the broad, tiled terrace of the Hotel Cecil. Ahead of her, a grey bulk showing dimly above the Riffian coast, was Gibraltar; to the left, a soft undulating sweep of Spanish hills; left and a little behind her, the white jumble of Tangier, one slim green minaret rising from the pleasing chaos of white and blue. The murmur of the awakened city came out to her and brought a little sense of exhilaration. Tangier was so much alive, so virile, so mysterious, so old – it was like a place in the Old Testament lit by electricity, a scrap of Babylon, if you could imagine Babylon with advertisements of absinthe plastered on the palace walls.

The sea was a gorgeous blue and motionless. Far away on the horizon, a great steamer, hull down, was making its way westward through the Staits. The sweet scent of mimosa came in soft puffs from a great golden bush near by.

She was alone on the terrace, but the table was laid for two. She had finished her breakfast, and her idle fingers played with a scrap of toast.

Her happiness was almost complete. For three months she had lived such a life as she had only pictured in her most exhilarated moments. The cities of the world which had existed for her only in pictures and in descriptions were now realities to her. Her feet had trod the floors of the Prado, had stood where Caesar stood in Rome, had climbed the steep hill to the Gate of the Sun in Toledo, had walked under Mont Blanc, had passed along the shaded pavements of Vienna.

She was perfectly happy, she told herself, yet instinctively made a reservation. What that reservation was she did not put into words, did not even mould it into thought. There was one little shadow.

She heard a firm footstep behind her and turned. It was her husband.

"Hallo, you're early!" he said.

She smiled a welcome to him, and he took her hand.

He sat on the other side of the table.

"I ordered my breakfast as I came," he said; "somehow I'm not hungry as I ought to be."

A look of alarm come into her eyes.

"You're not ill?" she said anxiously.

He smiled indulgently. "Oh, no, I'm not ill!"

"The porter was telling me," she went on, speaking quickly, almost incoherently, "there has been typhoid in Tangier. Don't you think we had better go away? I could pack my bags in time to catch the boat – "

He shook his head laughingly.

"Please don't worry, there is no cause."

"I couldn't have you ill here," she said, and shook her head doubtingly. "We could run over to Cadiz and go to Paris."

"I assure you," he began, then he stopped and frowned. "Typhoid in Tangier," he repeated her words; "by Jove, that's serious." He looked at her in a panic. "I think we'll go," he said, "it isn't worth taking a risk; I'd never forgive myself if you got ill."

She stopped him with a burst of ringing laughter. He saw the humour of the situation and laughed responsively.

"I suppose," he said, "there's typhoid everywhere, if one looks for it."

He sat down to the table and sorted over the pile of letters that awaited him. He opened one. It was in the flowing handwriting of Wentworth Gold. He scanned it eagerly.

"There's no news?" she asked.

"None of importance," he said. "Isn't it curious," he looked up from his letter, "that Gold, the least romantic of men, should ascribe Helder's death to a broken heart?"

"Poor man!" she said softly.

He pushed back his chair and looked absently across the yellow stretch of sand.

"He was rather a sinner," he said; "but who can tell the temptations to which such a man, ambitious and without influence, can be subjected? I can forgive him many things; to my mind, his forgeries were the least of his offences."

She was silent, knowing that his mind had gone back to that day in Helder's office when he had first spoken to her.

"No other letters?" she asked after a while.

He put down the letter he had been looking through with a little smile!

"The usual thing," he said dryly. "It is curious how people always want you to be happy in their way, and when they picture your happiness, imagine it under conditions entirely different from those you enjoy."

She looked up quickly, then lowered her eyes again.

"You are quite happy, aren't you?" she asked quietly.

"Quite," he said. There was no hesitation or doubt in his voice, but there was no depth in his tone either. The word "quite" was just a word without emphasis but without hesitation. It neither inferred perfection in happiness nor suggested anything to the contrary.

"As happy as you had expected?" She was playing with fire and she knew it, and was none the less happy in the risk she took.

"More," he said.

He looked down at her gravely: he had risen, and was leaning with his back to the stone parapet.

"Much more than I had ever hoped – you look a little troubled," he added quickly.

She smiled up at him.

"No, though sometimes I worry a little about the future. I have qualms of conscience. I feel that in some way I am standing between you and the best part of your life."

"You are the best part of my life," he said with a lowered voice; "whatever the future holds that is a present fact. It is so easy to love you, Verity."

The word were very simple, but there was in his tone sincerity which was beyond doubt.

She flushed, yet raised an empty coffee cup to her lips in an heroic effort to dissemble her agitation.

"Some day, in the years ahead," he went on, "love will come to you. It is worth waiting – "

"Suppose," she interrupted timidly, "suppose it never comes. Is it fair – to me – to depend so much on that?"

"If it does not come, something else equally as precious will come in its place."

She did not speak for a minute of two. She sat with her eyes fixed upon the cup before her, turning it round and round aimlessly.

"Suppose," she said, without raising her eyes, "we discover – that day – only suppose?"

He nodded.

"Suppose it was between us – as it should be – that love – real love – lived and flourished in both our hearts – should we go away on another trip like this, away from the world and people, just you and I?"

He did not trust himself to speak, he nodded again.

The twirling of the cup became faster and more furious as she went on.

"It's very tempting," she half whispered. "All that lovely trip over again. It tempts me to wait till we have settled down in England – "

The cup fell to the tiled floor of the terrace and broke into a hundred pieces. She laughed and rose quickly. Her colour came and went.

"But I am not going to wait!" she said.

EDGAR WALLACE

BIG FOOT

Footprints and a dead woman bring together Superintendent Minton and the amateur sleuth Mr Cardew. Who is the man in the shrubbery? Who is the singer of the haunting Moorish tune? Why is Hannah Shaw so determined to go to Pawsy, 'a dog lonely place' she had previously detested? Death lurks in the dark and someone must solve the mystery before BIG FOOT strikes again, in a yet more fiendish manner.

BONES IN LONDON

The new Managing Director of Schemes Ltd has an elegant London office and a theatrically dressed assistant – however Bones, as he is better known, is bored. Luckily there is a slump in the shipping market and it is not long before Joe and Fred Pole pay Bones a visit. They are totally unprepared for Bones' unnerving style of doing business, unprepared for his unique style of innocent and endearing mischief.

Edgar Wallace

Bones of the River

'Taking the little paper from the pigeon's leg, Hamilton saw it was from Sanders and marked URGENT. *Send Bones instantly to Lujamalababa… Arrest and bring to head-quarters the witch doctor.*'

It is a time when the world's most powerful nations are vying for colonial honour, a time of trading steamers and tribal chiefs. In the mysterious African territories administered by Commissioner Sanders, Bones persistently manages to create his own unique style of innocent and endearing mischief.

The Daffodil Mystery

When Mr Thomas Lyne, poet, poseur and owner of Lyne's Emporium insults a cashier, Odette Rider, she resigns. Having summoned detective Jack Tarling to investigate another employee, Mr Milburgh, Lyne now changes his plans. Tarling and his Chinese companion refuse to become involved. They pay a visit to Odette's flat. In the hall Tarling meets Sam, convicted felon and protégé of Lyne. Next morning Tarling discovers a body. The hands are crossed on the breast, adorned with a handful of daffodils.

Edgar Wallace

The Joker

While the millionaire Stratford Harlow is in Princetown, not only does he meet with his lawyer Mr Ellenbury but he gets his first glimpse of the beautiful Aileen Rivers, niece of the actor and convicted felon Arthur Ingle. When Aileen is involved in a car accident on the Thames Embankment, the driver is James Carlton of Scotland Yard. Later that evening Carlton gets a call. It is Aileen. She needs help.

The Square Emerald

'Suicide on the left,' says Chief Inspector Coldwell pleasantly, as he and Leslie Maughan stride along the Thames Embankment during a brutally cold night. A gaunt figure is sprawled across the parapet. But Coldwell soon discovers that Peter Dawlish, fresh out of prison for forgery, is not considering suicide but murder. Coldwell suspects Druze as the intended victim. Maughan disagrees. If Druze dies, she says, 'It will be because he does not love children!'

OTHER TITLES BY EDGAR WALLACE AVAILABLE DIRECT FROM HOUSE OF STRATUS

Quantity	£	$(US)	$(CAN)	€
THE ADMIRABLE CARFEW	6.99	11.50	15.99	11.50
THE ANGEL OF TERROR	6.99	11.50	15.99	11.50
THE AVENGER	6.99	11.50	15.99	11.50
BARBARA ON HER OWN	6.99	11.50	15.99	11.50
BIG FOOT	6.99	11.50	15.99	11.50
THE BLACK ABBOT	6.99	11.50	15.99	11.50
BONES	6.99	11.50	15.99	11.50
BONES IN LONDON	6.99	11.50	15.99	11.50
BONES OF THE RIVER	6.99	11.50	15.99	11.50
THE CLUE OF THE NEW PIN	6.99	11.50	15.99	11.50
THE CLUE OF THE SILVER KEY	6.99	11.50	15.99	11.50
THE CLUE OF THE TWISTED CANDLE	6.99	11.50	15.99	11.50
THE COAT OF ARMS	6.99	11.50	15.99	11.50
THE COUNCIL OF JUSTICE	6.99	11.50	15.99	11.50
THE CRIMSON CIRCLE	6.99	11.50	15.99	11.50
THE DAFFODIL MYSTERY	6.99	11.50	15.99	11.50
THE DARK EYES OF LONDON	6.99	11.50	15.99	11.50
THE DAUGHTERS OF THE NIGHT	6.99	11.50	15.99	11.50
THE DEVIL MAN	6.99	11.50	15.99	11.50
THE DOOR WITH SEVEN LOCKS	6.99	11.50	15.99	11.50
THE DUKE IN THE SUBURBS	6.99	11.50	15.99	11.50
THE FACE IN THE NIGHT	6.99	11.50	15.99	11.50
THE FEATHERED SERPENT	6.99	11.50	15.99	11.50
THE FLYING SQUAD	6.99	11.50	15.99	11.50
THE FORGER	6.99	11.50	15.99	11.50
THE FOUR JUST MEN	6.99	11.50	15.99	11.50
FOUR SQUARE JANE	6.99	11.50	15.99	11.50

ALL HOUSE OF STRATUS BOOKS ARE AVAILABLE FROM GOOD BOOKSHOPS
OR DIRECT FROM THE PUBLISHER:

Internet: www.houseofstratus.com including author interviews, reviews, features.

Email: sales@houseofstratus.com please quote author, title and credit card details.

OTHER TITLES BY EDGAR WALLACE AVAILABLE DIRECT
FROM HOUSE OF STRATUS

Quantity		£	$(US)	$(CAN)	€
	THE FOURTH PLAGUE	6.99	11.50	15.99	11.50
	THE FRIGHTENED LADY	6.99	11.50	15.99	11.50
	GOOD EVANS	6.99	11.50	15.99	11.50
	THE HAND OF POWER	6.99	11.50	15.99	11.50
	THE IRON GRIP	6.99	11.50	15.99	11.50
	THE JOKER	6.99	11.50	15.99	11.50
	THE JUST MEN OF CORDOVA	6.99	11.50	15.99	11.50
	THE KEEPERS OF THE KING'S PEACE	6.99	11.50	15.99	11.50
	THE LAW OF THE FOUR JUST MEN	6.99	11.50	15.99	11.50
	THE LONE HOUSE MYSTERY	6.99	11.50	15.99	11.50
	THE MAN WHO BOUGHT LONDON	6.99	11.50	15.99	11.50
	THE MAN WHO KNEW	6.99	11.50	15.99	11.50
	THE MAN WHO WAS NOBODY	6.99	11.50	15.99	11.50
	THE MIND OF MR J G REEDER	6.99	11.50	15.99	11.50
	MORE EDUCATED EVANS	6.99	11.50	15.99	11.50
	MR J G REEDER RETURNS	6.99	11.50	15.99	11.50
	MR JUSTICE MAXELL	6.99	11.50	15.99	11.50
	RED ACES	6.99	11.50	15.99	11.50
	ROOM 13	6.99	11.50	15.99	11.50
	SANDERS	6.99	11.50	15.99	11.50
	SANDERS OF THE RIVER	6.99	11.50	15.99	11.50
	THE SINISTER MAN	6.99	11.50	15.99	11.50
	THE SQUARE EMERALD	6.99	11.50	15.99	11.50
	THE THREE JUST MEN	6.99	11.50	15.99	11.50
	THE THREE OAK MYSTERY	6.99	11.50	15.99	11.50
	THE TRAITOR'S GATE	6.99	11.50	15.99	11.50
	WHEN THE GANGS CAME TO LONDON	6.99	11.50	15.99	11.50

Hotline: UK ONLY: 0800 169 1780, please quote author, title and credit card details.
INTERNATIONAL: +44 (0) 20 7494 6400, please quote author, title and credit card details.

Send to: House of Stratus Sales Department
24c Old Burlington Street
London
W1X 1RL
UK

Please allow for postage costs charged per order plus an amount per book as set out in the tables below:

	£(Sterling)	$(US)	$(CAN)	€(Euros)
Cost per order				
UK	1.50	2.25	3.50	2.50
Europe	3.00	4.50	6.75	5.00
North America	3.00	4.50	6.75	5.00
Rest of World	3.00	4.50	6.75	5.00
Additional cost per book				
UK	0.50	0.75	1.15	0.85
Europe	1.00	1.50	2.30	1.70
North America	2.00	3.00	4.60	3.40
Rest of World	2.50	3.75	5.75	4.25

PLEASE SEND CHEQUE, POSTAL ORDER (STERLING ONLY), EUROCHEQUE, OR INTERNATIONAL MONEY ORDER (PLEASE CIRCLE METHOD OF PAYMENT YOU WISH TO USE)
MAKE PAYABLE TO: STRATUS HOLDINGS plc

Cost of book(s): —————————— Example: 3 x books at £6.99 each: £20.97

Cost of order: —————————— Example: £2.00 (Delivery to UK address)

Additional cost per book: —————————— Example: 3 x £0.50: £1.50

Order total including postage: ————— Example: £24.47

Please tick currency you wish to use and add total amount of order:

☐ £ (Sterling)   ☐ $ (US)   ☐ $ (CAN)   ☐ € (EUROS)

VISA, MASTERCARD, SWITCH, AMEX, SOLO, JCB:

☐ ☐ ☐ ☐ ☐ ☐ ☐ ☐ ☐ ☐ ☐ ☐ ☐ ☐ ☐ ☐ ☐ ☐ ☐ ☐

Issue number (Switch only):

☐ ☐ ☐

Start Date: Expiry Date:

☐ ☐ / ☐ ☐   ☐ ☐ / ☐ ☐

Signature: _____

NAME: _____

ADDRESS: _____

_____

POSTCODE: _____

Please allow 28 days for delivery.

Prices subject to change without notice.
Please tick box if you do not wish to receive any additional information. ☐

House of Stratus publishes many other titles in this genre; please check our website (**www.houseofstratus.com**) for more details.